CASSANDRA DEAN

Finding Lord Farlisle

Lost Lords, Book One

By Cassandra Dean

Enslaved
Teach Me
Scandalous
Rough Diamond
Fool's Gold
Silk & Scandal
Silk & Scorn
Silk & Scars
Silk & Scholar
Slumber
Awaken
Finding Lord Farlisle
Rescuing Lord Roxwaithe

To my family and friends. You hold my hand and talk me down from the ledge.

And to F4E, AL Clark. I literally could not have done this without you. Thank you for bonding with me over Buffy all those years ago.

CASSANDRA DEAN

Finding Lord Farlisle

Lost Lords, Book One

Chapter One

Northumberland, England, August 1819

LIGHTNING STREAKED ACROSS THE darkening sky and thunder followed. Stillness held sway a moment, the air thick, before a torrent of rain battered the earth.

Wrestling against the wind, Lady Alexandra Torrence tucked her portmanteau closer to her person as she pushed determinedly toward the estate looming in the distance. The storm had been but a sun-shower when she'd set out from Bentley Close, her family's estate only a half hour walk. While the light cloak she wore protected her from the worst of it, the wet was beginning to seep into her skin.

She pulled her cloak tighter. It was only a little farther and she'd be at Waithe Hall, though there would be no one to greet her. Waithe Hall had been closed for years, ever since the previous earl had died. The new earl—Viscount Hudson, as he'd once been—resided almost exclusively in London. Her family and his had been close for as long as she could remember, their townhouses bordering each other in London just as their estates did here in Northumberland. The earl was her elder by nine years, and his brother Stephen by five, but Maxim, the youngest, had been but one year her senior and—

She stopped that thought in its tracks.

Before too much longer, she stood at the entrance to Waithe Hall, and with it, shelter. The huge wooden doors were shut. She could not recall that she had ever seen them closed and locked. In the past when she'd visited the family had been in residence so she would walk straight in, calling for Maxim before she'd completely cleared the entrance—

Slowly, she exhaled. After a moment, she pulled the key from her pocket, the one Maxim had given to her for safekeeping when he was ten and she nine, so they could always find their way back in should the doors ever be locked—

Shoving the key into the lock, she blinked fiercely as she forced memory aside once more. She could do this. It had been years, the wound so old it should have long since faded. She could investigate Waithe Hall and its ghosts, and she would not think of him.

The key turned easily, the door swinging open. She stepped inside. Cavernous silence greeted her, the din of the rain that had been so deafening now distant. The entrance stretched before her, disappearing into darkness, and the storm had made the late afternoon darker than usual, swallowing any light that peeked through closed doors. Pausing mid-step, she wondered if perhaps she had made a mistake in coming here.

Shaking off doubt, she started through the hall. The rain echoed through the vastness, the hollow sound strange after being caught in its fury. Fumbling through her portmanteau she found a candle and tinder.

The flickering light revealed an entrance corridor that opened into an enclosed court encompassing the first and second floors, and an impressive chandelier draped in protective cloth hung at its centre. Memory painted it with crystal and candles, and she remembered sitting on the landing of the second floor, legs dangling through the gaps between balusters as she and Maxim counted the crystals for the hundredth time.

Bowing her head, she cursed herself. She should have known she could not keep the memories at bay.

A roll of thunder reverberated around her, leaving behind quiet and dark. All her memories of Waithe Hall were full of life, the butler directing servants, fresh flowers in the vases lining the court, light spilling through from the mammoth windows. Now the windows were shuttered, and an eerie silence broken only by the sounds of the storm pervaded.

Hitching her bag, she made her way to the

sitting room. It was as still as the rest of the estate, the furniture draped in holland covers, the windows also shuttered. Setting her candle down, she placed her cloak over the back of a chair and rested her bag on its seat, glancing nervously about. She caught herself. *Don't be stupid, Alexandra. There's none here.*

Before she could think further, she unbuttoned her bodice. Her clothes were soaked, uncomfortably damp against her skin, and a chill was beginning to seep through, though it was the tail end of summer and the days were still mostly warm. She'd chosen a simple gown, one she knew she could get into and out of herself.

Heat rose on her cheeks as she shucked out of the bodice. There was none here. She *knew* there was no one. Cheeks now burning, she untied her skirt and petticoats, left only in her stays and chemise. She would love to remove her stays as well, but they were only slightly damp and she couldn't bring herself to disrobe more than she had.

Opening her bag, she pulled out a spare bodice, skirt, petticoats and, finally, a towel. Thanking her stars she'd had the forethought to bring it, she quickly swiped herself, chanting all the while there was no one watching her, that doing this in an abandoned sitting room was *not* immodest.

In record time, she'd managed to reclothe herself. Hanging her wet clothes to dry, she pushed her hair out of her face. Once she had explored further, she would choose one of the bedchambers as her base, but for right now the sitting room would suffice.

A thread of guilt wound through her. Technically, the earl did not know she was a guest of Waithe Hall—and by technically, she meant he didn't know at all. She was confident however, he could have no objection. She had been a regular presence at Waithe Hall when she was a girl, and the earl held some affection for her. She was almost positive. Maxim had often said his brother thought her—

Damnation. Bracing herself against a chair, she bowed her head. She had thought more of him in the last hour than she had in the year previous. It was this place. She'd managed to convince herself she no longer felt the sharp bite of grief, but she did. It struck her at odd moments, and she could never predict when. One would think it would have lessened with time, but it hit her fresh and raw, as if she bled all over again. She'd been a fool to think she would remain unaffected returning here—he was everywhere.

She closed her eyes as realisation cut through her. She was going to think of him. It was inevitable. However, she had come here with purpose and she would not allow this preoccupation to deter her.

The ghosts of Waithe Hall beckoned.

A darkening gloom shrouded the drawing room. Night approached, quicker than she'd liked, but she was determined to at least do a preliminary sweep of the estate to refresh her memory before it became too dark to continue. There was much to do before she camped out in the affected room one night soon, not the least of which was determining *which* room was affected.

From her bag, she pulled a compass, a ball of twine, and her notebook. Bending over the flickering light of her candle, she opened her notebook and dated the page, jotting down her notes on the expedition thus far.

There had always been tales of ghosts at Waithe Hall. On her and Maxim's frequent rides about the estate, she remembered listening wide-eyed as Timmons had told them tales of ghosts and woe. The groom had waxed lyrical on the myths and legends of spiritual activity at Waithe Hall, and she'd been completely fascinated. Maxim had never seemed interested, but he'd always followed when she'd concocted a new adventure to discover ghosts and ghouls. As an adult, she'd turned her fascination into a hobby, researching and cataloguing ghost tales at every manor and estate she'd attended. Her own family's estate held a ghost or two, stories her father had been only too happy to tell. She'd documented his tale and others, and had submitted several articles to the Society for the Research of Psychical Phenomena. They hadn't as yet chosen to publish any of them, but she was convinced if she persisted, eventually they would.

Then, four months ago, reports had crossed

the earl's desk in London of strange lights at Waithe Hall. He'd mentioned it in passing to her father, who in turn, knowing her fascination, had mentioned it to her. He'd also issued a stern warning she was not to pursue an investigation but, well, she was twenty-five years old and in possession of an inheritance a great aunt had left her. Her father could suggest, but he could not compel.

The lights could be any number of things, but the report had contained accounts of a weeping woman, and the light had become a search light. Memory reminded her of a tale Timmons had told, the lament of a housekeeper of Waithe Hall who had lost a set of keys and caused a massacre. Her lips quirked. Timmons' tales had ever been grisly.

Determination had firmed and within a week she'd made her way to Northumberland and Waithe Hall. Bentley Close had been shut as well, but unlike Waithe Hall, a skeleton staff kept the estate running. Along with her maid, Alexandra had arrived late last night though she hadn't been in a position to set out for Waithe Hall until late this afternoon. Her plan had always been to spend a few days here, but the rain made it that she now had no choice.

She would rather be here than in London anyway. Besides pretending she was unaffected by those who called her odd, her younger sister had finally made her debut at the grand old age of twenty. Lydia was taking society by storm, determined to wring every ounce of pleasure out of her season, and she had confidently informed their parents she didn't intend to wed until she had at least three seasons behind her. At first horrified, their parents had resigned themselves to neither of their daughters marrying any time soon.

As the eldest of her parents' children and a female besides, she had borne the brunt of their expectations in that respect, but at least Harry had now brought them some joy. He and Tessa Pike were to marry next year, the wedding of the heir to a marquessate and a duke's daughter already touted as the event of the season. George had absconded to the continent, no doubt investigating the most macabre medical reports he could, while Michael was still at Eton.

Upstairs, a door slammed shut. Alexandra jumped, hand flying to her racing heart. It was the wind. It had to be. Even now it howled outside, rain pelting the roof and echoing through the hall as distant thunder rolled.

Hugging the notebook to her chest, she shucked off any concerns. There was no time like the present. She would start with an examination of the ground floor. The kitchens and servants rooms would take an age, so better to examine the family rooms and save the servants for another time.

The portrait gallery was as she remembered, a long stretch of hall that displayed the Farlisles in all their permutations. Quickly, she traversed its length, telling herself the dozens of eyes of previous Farlisles did not follow her, that they did not judge her an unwelcome guest. Cold slid up her spine and she moved faster, especially as she passed the portrait of the old earl and his sons, Maxim staring solemnly from the portrait.

Pretending she felt not a skerrick of unease, she noted the gallery's dimensions in her diary and moved on to the second sitting room. Again, nothing in particular was out of the ordinary.

The library was at the end of the corridor, and the door opened easily under her hand. It really was most obliging of the steward not to have locked any of the doors inside the estate. This room was vastly different to her remembrance. Few books lined the shelves thick with dust, and holland covers draped most of the furniture, although one of the high-backed arm chairs before the fire was lacking the covering. Peculiarly, one of the windows here was unshuttered, the weak light of storm-dampened twilight casting eerie shadows on the wall opposite.

She'd always loved the library and its two storeys containing rows upon rows of books. As children, she'd insisted she and Maxim spend an inordinate amount of time within its walls, happily miring herself in book after book. Maxim had always been bored within seconds, spending his time tossing his ever-present cricket ball higher and higher in the air to see if he could hit the ceiling two floors above. He'd even managed it, a time or two.

Sharp pain lodged beneath her breast. Rubbing at her chest, she took a breath against it, pulling herself to the present. Somehow, night had encroached upon the room. How long had she been stood there, lost in memory?

Moving further into the room, she trailed her fingers over the side table next to the undraped chair. A stack of thick books was piled high, the top one containing a marker. Why was there a stack of books? Had an apparition placed them there?

A prickle rippled along her skin. She'd never seen a ghost. She'd heard hundreds, thousands of stories, but she'd never— Steadying herself, she flipped open the book to the spot marked, noting it was a history of the Roman invasion and settlement of Cumbria. Sections and rows were underlined with pencil, writing filled the margins, and there was something about the hand….

Closing the book, she placed it back on the stack. Why was this here? Every other part of Waithe Hall she'd seen had been closed, shut away. This room held an uncovered chair, a stack of books and…. The fireplace held recent ashes.

Her heart began to pound.

Again, something—a door?—banged. Whirling around, she searched the encroaching dark, her gaze desperate as her chest heaved. What if the lights weren't a ghost? What if it was a vagrant, someone dangerous and unkind? What if…what if it were a *murderer*?

The agitated sound of her breathing filled the room. Getting a hold of herself, she reined in her imaginations. Her thoughts could—and frequently did—run to the extreme. Although these anomalies were curious, there could be a perfectly mundane reason for their presence. There was nothing out of the ordinary, besides the books, and the fireplace, and—

She took a breath. *Calm, Alexandra.* She was purportedly an investigator. She would investigate.

The fireplace had without doubt been used recently. Newly cut logs placed in a neat pile to the side. Sconces held half-used candles, their wicks blackened and bodies streaked with melted wax. She could see no other signs of occupation—

Something banged for a third time, closer now, and brought with it a howling wind. Alexandra jumped, grabbing at the table for balance as the door to the library flew open, the heavy wood banging against the wall, the books wobbling and threatening to fall. Blood pounding in her ears, she looked to the darkened maw of the library's entrance.

An indistinct white shape filled the door, hovering at least five feet above the floor.

A scream lodged in her throat. She couldn't move, couldn't make a sound. She could only stare as the thing approached.

Lightning crashed, flashing through the

room. She gasped, a short staccato sound that did little to unlock her chest.

Lightning crashed again. The shape became distinct in the brief flash of light, revealing a man dressed in shirt sleeves and breeches, his dark hair long about his harsh face. A strong, handsome face that held traces of the boy she'd thought never to see again.

Blood drained from her own face, such she felt faint. "Maxim?"

Chapter Two

"WHAT ARE YOU DOING here?" it—he—growled.

"Maxim?" she repeated stupidly. The apparition before her looked so much like Maxim…if Maxim had grown to a man, developed an abundance of muscle and four inches of height. It couldn't be Maxim…but if it were an apparition, why would he appear grown? When last she'd seen him, he'd been fifteen and skinny as a reed, not much taller than she. It couldn't be him.

Lightning lit the room once more. His shirt was loose about his thighs, the ties undone and the neck gaping open, his breeches smudged with dirt. All was well tailored and untattered. Surely, if he were a ghost, his raiments should be tattered?

The same chestnut hair fell over his brow, too long and ragged, while his face had broadened and hardened, his eyes were the same, chocolate brown under dark brows. He'd grown to a man, broad shoulders and ropy muscle apparent behind the scant clothes he wore, his breeches stretched over powerful thighs and strong calves, his large feet shod in well-worn leather boots.

He was supposed to be dead. Eleven years ago, he had abruptly left Eton and set sail on one of the Roxwaithe ships, bound for America. She'd been so confused at the time, and he'd refused to tell her why. Six months later, they had received word the ship had been lost at sea. None had survived.

With startling clarity, she remembered that day. Her father's face, careworn and concerned, as he'd told her. Her mother's worried eyes. The pain in her chest, frozen at first, until she'd excused herself, blindly making her way to her chamber only to stand in its centre, confusion filling her until she'd happened to glance upon his cricket ball, the one he'd given her the last time she'd seen him, where he'd been worried about something but he'd refused to tell her what and yelled at her when she'd pressed him, and once she'd returned home she'd thrown it onto her dressing table, angry beyond belief at him, and then, then a great gaping hole had cracked open inside her and she'd slid to the floor, pain and grief and devastation growing inside her until it had encompassed all, it had encompassed everything and it hadn't stopped, it hadn't *stopped*, it—

It was eleven years ago. The pain had faded, but never truly left. She'd thought she'd learned to live with it. But now…he was here?

A thunderous scowl on his face, he made a noise of impatience. "I do not have the inclination for this, girl. Tell me why you have come."

His voice crashed over her. That, too, had deepened with age, but it was him. It was *him.*

"It *is* you." Joy filled her, so big it felt her skin couldn't contain it. Throwing herself at him, she enveloped him in a hug.

He stiffened.

Embarrassment coursed through her. What was she thinking? Immediately, she untangled herself from him. "I beg your pardon," she stammered. Always before they'd been exuberant in their affections. They'd always found ways to touch one another, even though that last summer, the one before he'd gone away, she'd begun to feel…more.

Clasping her hands before her, she brought herself to the present. Much had changed, now they were grown and he, apparently, had not died.

Maxim had not died.

A wave of emotion swept her, a mix of relief, joy, incredulity…. It buckled her knees and burned her eyes. He was alive. *Maxim was alive.*

"When did you return? Do your brothers know?" she asked, steadying herself as she swiped at the wetness on her cheeks. "The earl is lately in London, but I'm certain he would return should he know. My father will be so pleased to see, as will my mother. George and Harry will be beside themselves, and Lydia and Michael too, though they were so young when—" She cut herself off, barely able to say the word *died*. "We mourned you, Maxim."

He came closer. He'd grown so tall. When last she'd seen him, barely an inch had separated them, but now he was at least two hands taller. Faint lines fanned from his eyes, the tanned skin shocking in the cold English weather. Wherever he'd been, it had been sunburned.

"I ask again," he said. "Why have you come?"

Confusion drew her brows. "Maxim? Don't you remember me?"

Starting at the blonde hair piled limply on her head thanks to the rain, he ran his gaze over her. He traced her face, her throat, travelled over her chest, swept her legs. A tingling began within her, gathering low. She was suddenly aware of how her breasts pushed against the fabric of her chemise with every breath, of a pulse between her legs that beat slow, steady….

He raised his gaze to hers. Silence filled the space between them before, succinctly, "No."

It was like a punch to her belly. "It's me. Alexandra."

No reaction.

Oh. Oh, this hurt.

Lifting her chin, she managed, "I am Lady Alexandra Torrence, daughter of your neighbour, the Marquis of Demartine. We grew up together."

His expression did not change.

"Your father, the previous earl, and mine were like brothers."

He stared at her. "Previous earl?" he finally asked.

"Yes," she said. "Your father passed away some years ago. Your eldest brother is now earl."

Again, no change in expression. Did he not care his father had died? But what did she know of this new Maxim? Less than an hour ago, she had not known he was alive.

He continued to stare at her. She fought the urge to shift under that flat gaze. "Why are you here?" he repeated, his tone harsh and impatient.

"I was—" Her voice cracked. Cursing her nerves, she cleared her throat. "I am investigating. The villagers spoke of a ghostly presence, lights and wails, and I...." She trailed off. Lord, it made her sound so odd. He'd always teased her about that oddness, and always with affection. She didn't know what this new Maxim would do.

Finally there was expression on his face. She wished it had remained stony. "Ghosts? You have invaded my home for ghosts?"

The disgust in his voice made her cringe. "To be fair, I didn't know you were here. No one did."

Expression still disdainful, he didn't reply.

Irritation pushed aside devastation. How could he not remember *her*? "This is not *your* home."

His brows shot up. "*That* is your argument?"

He sounded so much like *her* Maxim. They'd argued often, and the number of times he'd said those exact words, in that exact tone…. She shook herself. "Yes. It is."

"A fallacy. You argue a fallacy."

"It is not a fallacy. It is objectively true. Waithe Hall is the ancestral seat of the Earls of Roxwaithe. You are not the Earl of Roxwaithe, ergo, it is not your home." Knowing it was childish, she tossed her hair and glared.

Crossing his arms, he scowled. "I know you are somewhere you don't belong."

"So are you," she pointed out.

"This is my family home."

"It's your *brother's*," she said. "You're being deliberately obtuse."

"And you're being obstinate."

"*I'm* being obstinate? Me?" This was such a ridiculous argument, and yet it was familiar. They'd argued like this all the time, and he was reacting exactly as *her* Maxim would react, and—

Stepping forward, he deliberately loomed over her. "I come into *my* library to find a trespasser, poking around in *my* things."

"Waithe Hall is shut. Roxwaithe hasn't been here in years. *No one* is supposed to be here. You aren't even supposed to be *alive*. How are you even *feeding* yourself?"

Pinching the bridge of his nose, he shook his head. "Why am I arguing with you? You're a trespasser I don't know."

Rage, such as she'd never experienced before, exploded. How dare he? How dare he pretend not to know her? Her fingers curled into fists and she told herself she could not punch him. She was a lady, and he was a *clodpole*. "Don't be *stupid*."

He stilled, and something flickered in his dark eyes. "You will leave the way you came."

"With pleasure," she snapped. Pushing past him, she stalked from the library, through the entrance hall, and wrenched the door open. Rain pelted her, almost horizontal as the wind howled and lightning crashed across the sky. She plunged into it, anger propelling her even as she was drenched in moments.

She'd not gotten more than two strides before a large hand grabbed her shoulder and hauled her back inside. Maxim slammed the door shut and shook himself, water falling to the marble floor. "Do you have any brains?" he demanded.

"You told me to go. I have no desire to say here with *you*."

"You wouldn't get half a mile before you'd catch your death. You'll stay here."

"It would not be proper," she said stiffly.

He laughed harshly. "Hunting a ghost is not proper, either. You will stay here."

Mutinously, she glared at him. Damnation. She could not even *argue* that point. Belatedly, she realised the rain had plastered his shirt to his body, clinging to hard muscle and broad shoulders.

Mouth abruptly dry, her breath locked in her chest.

He didn't seem to notice her distraction. "Come," he said, holding aloft a lamp he'd magically produced, before turning on his heel to stride down the corridor. Hesitantly, she followed.

They wound through the Hall, climbing the grand stairs and making their way to the family apartments, the corridors she remembered from her—their—childhood. Wrapping her arms about herself, she cursed herself at the soaked fabric. She'd only brought two gowns, and now both were wet.

He halted before a door. "You may stay here," he said, pushing it open.

Passing him, she entered a bedchamber, again with most of the furniture covered. The bed, though, was not, holding a mattress along with pillows and sheets.

Surprise filled her. "Is this where you sleep?"

He placed the lamp on the dresser. "Goodnight."

"Good—?" He was gone before she finished the word.

Wrapping her arms about her torso, she stopped herself from rushing after him. She wanted to assure herself she hadn't imagined him, that he was real, that he was alive...and she needed to get her bag, she had a nightgown and a change of underclothes, and—Maxim was alive.

Legs giving out, she collapsed onto the bed. The bed he had slept in, unmade with the sheets rucked to the foot of the bed. A faint scent wound about her, woodsy and indistinct, but she knew it was his, knew it was *Maxim's*. A harsh sob broke from her, and another, eleven years of emotion exploding. Sliding from the bed, she pulled herself into a ball, hot forehead against her updrawn knees, her cheeks wet, her chest hurting, her sodden clothes feeling as if they weighed a hundred pounds.

The wind howled, rain pelting the window. They'd all thought him dead. *She'd* thought him dead. Her dearest companion, her best friend. Maxim.

Slowly, her sobs subsided. She couldn't stay here. She couldn't take his bed from him, and she.... She wanted to know. She wanted to know everything. Why was he here? Why hadn't he gone to his brothers? Why was he lurking in Waithe Hall alone? When had he returned?

Did he really not remember her?

Taking a shuddering breath, she wiped at her cheeks. She needed to know and surely he would tell her. Even if he didn't remember her.

Rising to her feet, she squared her shoulders. Well, she would make him remember her...and then she would make him let her hug him.

Chapter Three

ENTERING THE LIBRARY, MAXIM stripped his sodden shirt from his body. His breeches were soaked through, and his hair dripped cold water down his naked back. He crouched before the fireplace. It took seconds to arrange the logs and kindling, and even less to light them. These last days of summer were still warm, but the nights had started to cool, especially when one had chased a fool of a girl into a torrential downpour. Bending his head, he closed his eyes as the warmth from the fire stripped some of the chill from his skin, though his breeches remained uncomfortably damp.

Rising, he took the blanket that covered him most nights from the armchair before the fire and wound it about himself. There was little he could do about the damp breeches, seeing as the girl occupied the room where he kept his clothing, but he could at least warm himself. Chasing the girl into the storm had been all kinds of idiotic, but he couldn't in good conscience have allowed her to flit through the wilds of Northumberland in the middle of a lightning storm. Storms were rare in this part of the world, and the combination of darkness, unusual weather, uneven ground, and the torrent of rain would have no doubt brought about ruin.

Sinking into the chair, he stared at the fire as it popped and crackled, throwing light and heat around the room. For five months, he'd made his home here, occupying himself with maintaining the estate, fixing anything he found broken, keeping the grounds from becoming overgrown. If he needed food, he'd walk to the next village over and trade services for supplies. He'd narrowly avoided the steward a time or two, and no doubt the man was somewhat surprised at the continued good condition of the estate.

Waithe Hall held his strongest memories, and it was where he'd headed as soon as he'd gathered the resolve to return to the life of his youth. His memories were still muddy, and most likely he would never remember all he had lost, but when he'd walked the drive, seen Waithe Hall in the distance, recognition had hit him like a whip. His knees had buckled as a weight of a thousand remembrances almost felled him, and he'd been torn between running toward the house and running far, far away.

He'd remembered tussling with his brothers in the nursery rooms, chasing and being chased across the dales, playing cricket on warm, lazy days. He'd remembered summer light glinting off golden hair, a girl's laugh, the smell of warm grass, the chill of the lake against sun-hot skin. He'd remembered his father's cold anger that last day, the day he'd arrived home from Eton.

Unseeingly, he stared into the flames. When he'd discovered Waithe Hall had been shuttered, that his father and brothers were not in attendance, he'd been equal parts disappointed and relieved. He hadn't magically improved while in America and he'd dreaded confronting his father, seeing again the anger and disappointment in his expression, the failure of having a half-wit for a son. Now, however, it appeared he would never see his father's face again.

He pressed the heel of his hands against his burning eyes. He didn't know why he believed the girl, but he did. His father was dead. Another thing he'd lost. This nightmare would never end, would it? His father had not been a warm man, but he'd been his father. He should feel more than just a distant grief, shouldn't he?

The books stacked high on the side table mocked him. His father would laugh if he could see him now. Every evening, he opened one and tried to force the words to make sense. He underlined phrases and made notes, his writing barely legible, and he was certain he transposed letters, wrote them backwards, generally proved his doltishness with each pencil stroke.

Damn it, who was he trying to fool? He

couldn't bloody read, and he stayed at Waithe Hall because he didn't have the spine to face what remained of his family. He had no doubt by now his brothers knew what their father and he had fought about, knew their youngest brother was a dunce, and he couldn't face the brief joy of their reunion fading to chagrin and disappointment when they learned nothing had changed.

He rubbed his brow. Damn it, he couldn't relax. The uneasy peace he'd found in this place had been broken. Besides useless thoughts of his family, he couldn't forget that upstairs, the girl slept.

He'd misrepresented when he'd said he didn't remember her. He hadn't remembered her name, or that she was the daughter of a marquis, or that her family's estate bordered his, but he'd looked at her and known she loved lemon cakes and trifle. He'd known her shriek as a frog was slipped down the back of her dress. He'd known how her eyes brightened as she concocted a plan of mischief. He'd known her smell, her laugh, that her yellow hair shone gold in sunlight. He hadn't known her, but pieces of her were burned into him.

When first he'd seen her, just visible in the gloom of the library, he'd faltered. After years of ephemeral memory, suddenly she was real. He'd been convinced he'd concocted this girl, that she couldn't possibly exist in real life, and then she was before him, older but the same.

After the wreck, it had been months before he'd remembered more than his first name. Everything had been strange and out of order, flashes of memory that seemed real for a moment only to disappear just as quickly. He'd remembered he was Maxim, but not that he was the son of an earl. He'd remembered his brothers, but only that they numbered two and were older. He'd known he wasn't from the Americas, but only because he spoke differently to those around him. Slowly, his memory had returned, but there was always going to be parts that never did.

A quiet snick sounded, but he paid it no mind as he leaned his head back against the high-backed chair. Unused to the company of others, it took him a moment to realise the sound was the opening of the library door. Turning in his seat, he found the girl—Lady Alexandra—stood hesitantly on its threshold.

He scowled. "What do you want?"

She lifted her chin. "I cannot in good conscience allow you to surrender your bed to me. I was quite prepared to sleep rough tonight, and just because I was not expecting the Hall to be occupied will not change that."

Goddamn, she was annoying. Was she always so annoying? She'd assumed the bedchamber was his and he hadn't corrected her assumption. It wasn't wholly incorrect, as most nights he slept in the library, whatever book he'd chosen to torture himself with open in his lap. "I will not take the bed."

Expression turning mutinous, she said, "Well, neither will I." She flopped into the covered chair beside him, ignoring the dust that showered her at the move, and proceeded to glare.

Part of him admired her gall, even as the rest of him was wholly annoyed.

As he settled back in his seat to return her glare, the blanket he wore slipped. Her gaze dropped to his exposed bare chest, her eyes widening. Drawing in a sharp breath, she jerked her gaze back up as her breasts rose faster. Darkened eyes met his briefly before she glanced away, her cheeks red.

Did this girl.... Had she just regarded him lustfully? An answering heat rose sharply in him, tightening his groin, shortening his breath, and taking him completely unaware. "You should not be here," he said, angry at his body's reaction. "You don't know what dangers you court."

Startled eyes met his and then, unaccountably, she laughed. Genuine joy filled the sound, her expression almost fond.

Something in his chest loosened. He remembered that laughter.

"For all that you are different, you are still Maxim," she said.

"That doesn't mean anything. I could have changed drastically. I *have* changed drastically."

She shook her head. "You are still Maxim. Dark pronouncements and promises of dire consequence." Her smile brightened. "Maxim."

That something dislodged in his chest, spreading warmth. He scowled.

Silence fell between them, broken by the crackle of the fire and the howl of the wind. Ignoring her, he stared hard into the flames. When he'd arrived, the silence had unnerved him, with not even the distant click of a clock ticking to break it. As a boy, he remembered lying in his bed, his hands laced over his stomach as he'd listened to the servants moving about their duties, the clock ticking in the distance. Before, he'd loved his window open, so the sounds of the night had filled the air.

Now there were no servants, the clocks were silent, and he hadn't opened a window in years.

"What happened to you?"

Her quiet words broke the silence. Still staring at the flames, he smiled without mirth. Too much had happened to him.

When he didn't answer, she sighed softly. "You don't have to tell me anything, Maxim, but I am here, should you wish to."

A lump rose in his throat. He shook his head, desperate to be rid of it. He hadn't survived by being soft. He couldn't allow her to make him soft. He didn't know her. She was merely one of his memories, hazy and indistinct.

Levelling his gaze upon her, he said, "You are no one to me. Why should I tell you a thing?"

The girl's—Alexandra's—face collapsed. Something twinged inside, but he held on to his stony expression.

Before his eyes, she rebuilt herself. "Be that as it may, I remember you. I cannot put aside the affection I have for you, or the relief that you are yet alive. I am sorry if this makes you uncomfortable. I can only imagine what you have been through, and what you must still suffer to be shut up here in Waithe Hall without a single soul knowing of your existence."

She was so admirable. The twinge grew, but he maintained his stoniness. "How do you know I have not told my brothers of my return?"

"You did not know your father had passed away and your brother is now the earl. Besides, your brother would have told my father." She cocked her head. "I told you. Our families are close."

"You know nothing, girl." He told himself to ignore her. If he did it for long enough, surely she would go away. That it had never happened before did not mean it wouldn't happen now.

His brows drew. How did he know what she always did? Vague memories dredged though his mind, of a younger girl with a stubborn set to her chin glaring at him loftily while intense frustration rioted through him.

"I am only one year younger, you know."

Her words snapped him from his thoughts. "Pardon?"

"You shouldn't keep calling me girl. We're practically the same age."

"What does that have to do with anything?"

She rolled her eyes. *"Everything.* It has *everything* to do with it. You used to love lording that whole extra year over me, as if it means anything."

"It does mean something. It means I know more than you."

"How, pray tell, does it mean you know more?"

He smirked. "I have been alive a whole extra year."

A strange expression crossed her face, and, eyes bright, she quickly glanced away.

"Are you alright?" he asked suspiciously.

"Yes," she said, the word muffled.

He had a horrible feeling she was lying, but he wasn't going to question it.

They fell silent, staring at the fire as the wind continued to howl, and, strangely, he felt content.

***

MAXIM WOKE WITH A start. The fire had burned to embers, glowing gently in the dark. Outside, all was quiet.

He looked over. The girl—Alexandra—slumbered, her wrist bent awkwardly as her hand supported her head.

He stared at her. She was…odd. No one had cared about him for so long, it was strange this girl he half-remembered felt so strongly for him.

Rising, he approached her. She didn't move.

Gently, he prised her hand away. She frowned, moaning a little as she moved her undoubtedly sore neck. Laying her arm about his shoulders, he placed an arm at her back and beneath her knees before lifting her. She was light in his arms, her body turning into his as he manoeuvred around the armchairs.

Leaving the library, he climbed the stairs for the room she thought was his. The covers of the bed were in the same jumble as when last he'd left them. Gently he lowered her onto them and she sighed, stretching as she turned into the pillow to embrace it. The move pulled the bodice of her gown tight over her breast, outlining the soft roundness. Swallowing, he followed the curve of her hip, the nip of her waist, the way the gown clung to her legs, one hitched higher than the other. A lock of golden hair rested on her cheek and he smoothed it behind her ear, savouring the soft silkiness of her skin.

Abruptly, he realised what he was doing. He pulled from her, his fingertips burning.

She still wore her boots. He removed them, and covered her with a blanket, doing his utmost to not touch any portion of her skin. Job completed, he turned on his heel and strode from the room, resolving to forget how she looked in his bed.

Returning to the library, he stoked the embers until they once again caught flame, and then settled in to pass another night as he had all the others. Alone.

Chapter Four

Sunlight beat against Alexandra's closed eyelids. Frowning, she threw an arm over her face.

Confused, she opened her eyes and rose on her elbows, glancing down her body. Why was she wearing a dress instead of her nightgown?

Oh. She was in Waithe Hall. It had rained.

Maxim.

Jerking up, she blew at the hair that fell in her face. She hadn't imagined him, had she? Last she remembered, she'd been in the library and he'd been in the chair beside her. He'd fallen asleep first and she'd spent the longest time watching him, tracing the lines of his face, marvelling that he was here with her, that he was *alive*. She remembered that. She remembered him. Surely it couldn't have been an imagining?

Pushing her hair into some semblance of order, she jumped out of the bed. Her dress was twisted about her and horribly wrinkled, but she did her toilette as best she could. She never had retrieved her portmanteau, so this was as good as she was going to get.

Rushing through the corridor and down the stairs, her feet were sure as she made her way to the library. Most of her childhood had been spent within these walls, and she knew the way like it was her own home. All but one of the windows were still shuttered, murky light from the still stormy sky flooding the room. The library itself, though, was empty, the fireplace void of ashes. The stack of books had also disappeared.

Unease licking through her, she frowned. She *hadn't* imagined him.

Her stomach rumbled, reminding her she hadn't eaten since luncheon yesterday, and she was halfway to the kitchens before she realised she'd even started, her feet picking the path without her conscious direction. They'd spent an inordinate amount of time in the kitchen, she and Maxim, pestering Mrs Potter for treats fresh from the oven. The kitchens were as empty as the rest of Waithe Hall, but a collation of bread, cheese and hardboiled eggs sat on a plate on the table. A pot of tea stood beside it, along with a chipped teacup.

She hadn't imagined him. Maxim was *alive*.

Indescribable joy burst through her. Smiling hugely, she poured a cup of tea. He must have brought her to the bedchamber while she slept. She'd *told* him she didn't wish to take his bed and he'd given it to her anyway. He'd always been amazing at ignoring anything that didn't fit with what he thought should happen. That, as well, appeared not to have changed.

Taking a sip of the tea, she winced. It had steeped too long, becoming lukewarm and bitter, but surely food would combat the taste.

As she munched on the bread, she wandered the kitchens. Hidden behind some tarp in the storeroom were supplies: bread, potatoes, some dried meats, as well as a large container of tea and...sugar! Gratefully, she dumped a teaspoon in her cup, and then another for good measure.

Sipping, she considered the stores before her. Clearly, Maxim had been here for some time. How had he avoided detection? He must get supplies from the village, and it wasn't beyond the realms of possibility the villagers wouldn't recognise him. In any event, the steward checked the estate twice a month, and sent detailed reports to the earl. She knew this because she hadn't wanted the steward or the earl to know she intended to...*study* Waithe Hall.

Teacup halfway to her lips, she paused. Reports of the ghost could, in actuality, be Maxim.

Shaking herself, she shoved disappointment aside. She didn't know for a fact there was no ghostly activity. It could be a combination, or wholly spiritual in nature. Nothing had changed since she'd set out from London, apart from Maxim being alive.

Pleasantly full from the breakfast he'd left

her, she set out to find him.

It astonished her how well she remembered Waithe Hall. It had been almost a decade since last she'd been here, and yet she was sure-footed as she searched its corridors and rooms. Rain still fell, so she imagined he wouldn't be outside. She wasn't going anywhere, either. When she'd started out yesterday, she'd done so on foot and now she was stranded here until the rain broke.

The portrait gallery was absent of him, as were the drawing rooms and the study. The conservatory, however, was not.

Rain lashed the glass-panelled walls, the light moody and indistinct. Weaving through the greenery, Maxim effortlessly carried a large sack on his shoulder. Again, he wore no waistcoat or jacket and his shirt was open at the neck, baring a vee of golden skin. He strode past without noticing her presence. Her mouth dried as she watched the play of muscles in his back, her fascinated gaze raking every inch of him. She'd seen men haul items about, but never a man of Maxim's station. The abundance of well-developed muscle now made sense.

She followed him through the conservatory, the winding path leading to a single step that took one down a level, and then further to the next step that signalled the third and final level. Water covered the tiled floor, and he sloshed through it with no concern, dumping the sack before the door to the garden outside. Sweat plastered his shirt to his skin, and her avid gaze ran over him as she watched him stretch.

Dear god, what was she doing? Heat burned her cheeks as she averted her eyes. How could she regard him so, as if he were solely a body...even though it was a magnificent body. He was more than his form. He was funny, and brave, and smart, and they talked about everything and...and...and she couldn't believe he had changed much from who he'd been, even though it had been over a decade.

Clasping her hands before her, she cleared her throat.

He whipped around, his eyebrows lifting with surprise only to descend into a thunderous scowl when he spied her. Deliberately, he turned his back and continued arranging sacks before the door.

Intimidation rarely worked on her, and certainly not with *Maxim*. Lifting her chin, she said, "Good morning."

He grunted, which she supposed was a greeting.

"Did you sleep well?" she asked, finding it absurd she was discussing inanities with *Maxim*.

"Fine." Bending, he hefted a sack into the row before the door.

Good lord. The move pulled his breeches tight against strong thighs and a well-formed backside. "Uh, good. That's good. I mean—" Her cheeks burned. *Alexandra, get a hold of yourself.* "I slept well, too, but you shouldn't have deposited me in the bed."

"You looked awkward in the chair," he said, lifting another sack.

"No more than you."

He shrugged.

She wracked her brains for something further to say. "This rain appears to have set in. How long do you think it shall continue?"

He didn't respond, instead arranging the sacks in rows on top of each other against the door to the gardens. The sacks must contain sand. She recalled them from the infrequent occasions when the conservatory had flooded, but then it had been groundsmen hauling the sacks from the cellar to the conservatory, not a son of the house.

"I cannot recall the last time we saw such rain," she said, seemingly only able to converse in trivialities. "And a lightning storm as well. The last I remember is that autumn it rained every afternoon for three weeks. I thought I should go mad, being trapped inside."

He continued to arrange the sacks.

"We ended up investigating Bentley Close from one end to another. We were looking for Black Douglass's treasure map."

He stilled, his hand resting on a sack.

She continued to prattle. "Black Douglass was what we decided my great, great, great grandfather was called. He looked so fearsome in his portrait, do you remember?" She stroked her jaw. "He had that great, bushy, black beard, and a wicked scar across his face. He would take to the high seas on your ancestor's ships, pillaging gold

and jewels from the four corners of the earth."
Waving an imaginary sword, she grinned as she
recalled the tale. "Then he returned home to
Northumberland and fell madly in love with a
local lass. He gave up his dastardly ways, but his
treasure was hidden somewhere on the estate, and
he left behind a map for his descendants to
discover if they had only the courage to look."

He stared down at the sacks. "You always
insisted he gave up piracy for love," he finally
said.

Delighted he remembered, she said, "That's
because he did."

He snorted.

"Anyway, we were convinced it was
somewhere in the east wing. We had to dodge
Harry and George."

"Your brothers."

"They were ever so troublesome, always
underfoot."

"Your father caught us rummaging through
the attic and yelled at us something fierce."

The memory made her wince. "He was not
pleased, was he?"

He dug his hands into one of the sacks and
said nothing further.

Frustration bit her. She shouldn't push him.
She had no experience with a person who'd
experienced what he had—lost to his family and
then returned years later—but she wanted so
desperately for him to admit he remembered her,
remembered *them*.

Exhaling, she reined herself in. "The library was empty this morning."

His shoulders tensed, but he didn't respond.

"The books were gone and the fireplace was empty of ashes," she tried again.

"Most mornings I clear the room," he finally said. "There is usually nothing for the steward to discover."

It was like drawing blood from a stone. When they were children, they could not stop talking, a torrent of words spilling from them both whether it had been a day or a month since last they'd spoken. She knew he'd been gone too long, that much now divided them, but he was *Maxim*. How could they have changed so completely?

"Where have you been, Maxim?" she asked quietly.

His hands tightened. "Everywhere. Nowhere."

Well, that was a nothing answer. "Is that anywhere in particular?" she asked, irony heavy in her tone.

The corner of his mouth lifted.

Shock froze her. She'd actually made him smile? Stepping forward, she ignored the water sloshing over her boots and dampening the hem of her gown as she placed her hands over his.

He didn't shake her off, his fingers flexing beneath hers. They were big, rough, covered with calluses. A strange warmth filled her, rushing from her hand to her arm to her breasts, settling low in her belly.

Staring down at their hands, he said, "You cannot return home."

She blinked. "I beg your pardon?"

Glancing at the rain battering the conservatory glass, he said, "You cannot return home."

"Oh. No, I suppose I cannot."

"The marquis and marchioness will worry."

The rain really was quite torrential. "They are not in residence."

His gaze whipped around. "What?"

"My parents are in London."

His gaze felt like a brand. "And your siblings?"

"With my parents. Apart from George. He's on the Continent, no doubt causing mayhem."

Expression again growing thunderous, he ground out, "You are here by yourself?"

"I brought my maid."

A muscle worked in his jaw. "She is not here."

"I was never going to bring her *here*. She's at Bentley Close."

"You are telling me your parents allowed you to travel north, by yourself, a journey that lasts four days, to arrive at an estate that is partially staffed with your only protection being your maid?"

"Yes?" This display of emotion from him was astounding. This is what brought his emotion? "How do you know Bentley Close is partially staffed?"

Ignoring her, he balled his hands against his hips and hung his head. His lips moved.

"What are you doing?" she said.

"I'm counting," he gritted out.

"Why?"

"So I don't shake you."

Her brows shot up. "I beg your pardon?"

"You've flitted across the countryside with no thought to your safety. You enter a deserted manor, are stranded by a lightning storm, and you pursue a discourse with a strange man."

"You are not strange." Irritation swirled. "And I am not a fool, Maxim."

"No, you are merely thoughtless."

"I am not that, either."

"You don't know what harm can befall you. There are evil men out there. Women too."

"I know this," she said stiffly.

"No you don't!" He slammed his hand against his thigh. "You cannot know. *I* didn't know. I wandered blindly into trouble, time and again, and you—" He took a breath. "There are bad men out there," he said darkly.

"I am not a fool," she repeated.

Scowling, he moved forward, crowding her. "What are you doing here?"

Craning her neck, she met his thunderous gaze. He'd grown so, and apparently he thought he could use his height to intimidate her. "I told you. I am here to investigate spiritual activity."

He advanced again and she squared her

shoulders, refusing to budge.

The only sound was the pelt of rain against glass. The air between them grew heated. Chest tightening, she was acutely aware of how close they were, how if she stepped forward she would be in his embrace. Tongue darting out, she wet the corner of her mouth and his gaze dropped to her lips, his eyes darkening, and she held her breath, wanting him closer, wanting his mouth on hers, wanting him....

"Ah hell," he said, and then he kissed her.

Chapter Five

SURPRISE HELD HER MOTIONLESS. The arm about her waist drew her closer as his lips moved over hers, firm and demanding. Heat streaked through her and she opened to him, gasping as his tongue licked at her upper lip. Somehow, she'd grasped his shirt and it crumpled as her hands tightened. She could feel his heart beating wildly against her knuckles. A moan built in her, and she wanted to be closer to him, to have him so close she never lost him again, that he would be with her always.

Suddenly he was gone, his back to her, his shoulders heaving. "You should not be here," he repeated darkly.

She raised her hand to her lips. She'd been kissed before, but never like that. Not like he would die if he didn't. "What was that for?"

He stilled. "You had to know."

"Know what?"

"There are bad people out there." Emotions played over his features before he ducked his head. "I am sorry."

She lowered her hand. "What are you sorry for?" she asked in a more normal tone.

"For…that." He waved his hand in her general direction.

"You're going to have to be more specific."

Raising his head, he met her gaze. Guilt painted his features.

Realisation pierced her. "Oh," she said in a small voice. Had he really kissed her to teach her a lesson?

"I am sorry," he repeated.

Beside the fact it was grossly condescending and supremely idiotic, the first time he'd kissed her had been because he'd thought to teach her a *lesson*. She wasn't ready to address the hurt, so she allowed anger to grow.

"I am truly sorry," he said again. "I should not have done so. It was ungentlemanly of me and…. I was wrong. I apologise."

"You kissed me as a lesson."

His cheeks ruddied. "It started that way, but I—It—"

Anger and heartache warring within her. "A lesson, Maxim? I do not require a lesson. I am well aware this world holds dangers and horrors. My best friend disappeared when I was almost fifteen years old and we all thought him dead. I thought I had died with him. I could not breathe for the hole in my chest. I learned to smile, and I learned to laugh, but that hole remained. Reports came, of privateers and shipwrecks, and suddenly the world was filled with peril and treachery. The world had taken you from me, Maxim." Tears burned behind her eyes. "I have long been aware this world is not safe."

"I apologise," he said softly.

She closed her eyes briefly. It had happened. Neither of them could change it. "Thank you."

"Are you going to undertake your investigation?" he asked just as softly.

Grateful for the change in topic, she said, "I believe I shall."

"May I join you?"

Conflicting emotion warred. "I don't know...." Did she even want him to come? But over and above, he was still Maxim, for all that he'd made a move wrong-headed and dumb.

No expression crossed his face. "I can assist. I can carry heavy objects, hold your notebook when you do not require it, measure distances. If you require a second pair of eyes, mine are available."

Macabre suggestions popped into her head and amusement tugged at her. "Can you remove them from your head?" she asked, as seriously as she could manage.

Clearly thrown by her question, his brow creased. "I beg your pardon?"

"The second pair of eyes. Can you remove them? Maybe I could keep them in my pocket."

His lips twitched. "Though you would look strange with brown eyes," he said, just as seriously.

She nodded gravely. "Hazel has been my eye colour of choice until now."

He ducked his head, but not before she saw the half-smile on his lips.

Triumph rose, that she had managed to make him smile again. Clearing her throat, she said, "You may assist me, but you understand you must undertake my direction?"

He nodded once, sharply.

"Good. We shall investigate the north-facing rooms on the second floor first."

"Really? Why?"

"They are the rooms facing the village. All the reports came from the village."

He nodded again. "Do you remember the way?"

"Of course."

"You're going to go up the main staircase, aren't you?"

"I—" She closed her eyes. Oh. She had forgotten. Opening her eyes, she found him looking at her with an expression one could almost term smug, if one were generous and discounted that his features were often inscrutable. "It's rude to smirk."

"I have no issue with you taking the stairs," he said. "I'll meet you there, shall I?"

"Maxim."

"Such a novelty: someone else possessing a faulty memory."

She looked at him sharply. His smile was

almost a grin, and in that moment, he seemed so like *her* Maxim. Averting her gaze, she bit her lip against the roiling tide inside her. "Where is it?"

"Just outside the conservatory. Come." He held out his elbow and she took it, curling her hand around the hard, unyielding muscle of his bicep, his shirt damp from the sandbags and his work.

Lifting her skirts, she grinned. "Let us traverse a secret passage."

***

SECRET PASSAGES RIDDLED WAITHE Hall. Some were hewn into the rock, some were rickety wooden structures, some were less than three feet, and others wound almost the entire length of the Hall. They linked floors, servants' quarters to the family bedrooms, the kitchen to the mews. They were a variety of styles, as if each earl of Roxwaithe added his own passage along with a section of the Waithe Hall. Family lore had it the Jacobites found them useful, as did the Catholics, and every rebellion Roxwaithe had ever felt sympathy towards.

As children, she and Maxim had delighted in discovering each one, keeping tally in her ever-present notebook, the same notebook in which Maxim had drawn pictures, silly doodles that had made her giggle. Over the years, she'd filled countless notebooks, all locked in a chest in her bedroom in London. The ones featuring Maxim's drawings were close to the top, for when she had particularly missed him.

The passage from the corridor outside the conservatory to the hall on the second floor was of wooden construction, the staircase fairly sturdy despite its obvious age. They reached the top of the stairs and she followed Maxim as he confidently negotiated the narrow corridor, the lamp he held lighting the way.

He stopped, pressing a hand against the wall. She waited, but nothing happened.

"Is it—"

"It's here," he said. He pressed something and a panel slid open. Standing aside, he beckoned her. She passed by, glancing at him as she did so. He remained expressionless. She didn't know why she was surprised.

Entering the room, she looked around. It was the earl's bedchamber, the room large and airy, though like all the other rooms the furniture was draped in holland covers. Large windows looked over the gardens and, on a clear day, the chimney pots of Waithe Village could be seen in the distance.

"I remember this," Maxim said suddenly.

Alexandra jumped almost a foot. "Don't scare me like that!"

Unrepentant, he continued, "I remember traipsing around after you."

"Oh. Well. Good."

"You don't understand." Though his expression was neutral, his eyes were alight. "I *remember.* I didn't remember anything, not for the longest time."

"Congratulations." Was that harsh? It seemed harsh, but then he had kissed her as a *lesson*.

A scowl drew his features. He looked like a sullen child. A tall child with obscenely large muscles, and sulky full lips, and…she was stopping right there, thank you very much.

Certain her cheeks were red, she moved further into the room. There was nothing obvious that could be attributed to spiritual activity, but perhaps it was only at a certain time of night, or year, or…. She frowned. Rain lashed the window. What if the storm affected it?

Arms crossed, Maxim leaned his hip against what must be the dresser. "Are you setting out to prove it?"

"Prove what?"

He gestured. She wasn't sure at what. "Your ghost."

The mantelpiece contained an inlay of mother-of-pearl. Perhaps it shone in the moonlight? "I am not looking for proof. I am looking to discount every other possibility. Once that is done, whatever remains must be the truth."

"Very scientific of you."

"It *is* a science." The sketch of the fireplace in her notebook looked slightly off. Oh well, she'd never been much good at pictures. "Would you take my notebook?"

He recoiled. "Why?"

What a strange reaction. "Because I need to take measurements and it will be easier if you write them for me."

Shoulders hunched, he took the notebook from her.

She measured the facing width of mantelpiece first. "Facing width, three foot, seven inches."

Brows drawn in concentration, he stabbed at her notebook.

"Mantel, five foot, two inches."

And again. She repeated for each measurement. Regarding the fireplace, she said, "I think I am finished."

He surrendered her notebook with something like relief.

She squinted at the page. The scratches he'd made could be numbers and letters. "You never could write neatly."

Cheek turned toward her, he set his jaw. "This is frivolous."

Surprised at the turn of thought, she asked, "What do you mean?"

"We are doing this simply because it brings us pleasure." He made a circular gesture with his hand. "Frivolous."

"It is serious." In her ears, a hundred other voices—friends, acquaintances, society at large—chanted the same chorus, *frivolous, frivolous, frivolous*. "*I* am serious about this."

"I mean no offence. My days have been working from dawn until dusk. This is…different."

"It *is* work." The chorus grew louder, adding her sister, her parents, her brothers.

He cocked his head. "Is it, though?"

"It is *my* work."

"Hmm."

"What?" she demanded

"I didn't say anything," he said.

"No, you just scoffed."

"Scoffed? I did no such thing."

"Yes, you did, because you just did it."

"If I did—and I am in no way agreeing that I did—then you should—" The strangest expression came over his face. He didn't continue.

"Should what?" she asked impatiently.

A full smile lit his face, turning him from darkly handsome to stunningly beautiful. The chorus could not compete with such splendour and she drew in her breath sharply, her heart beating wild.

He shook his head, still smiling, oblivious to the impact he'd had on her.

"What?" she managed.

"Banter," he said.

"I beg your pardon?"

"We were bantering."

"We were arguing," she argued.

"Nevertheless. I haven't done that in…" Thoughtfully, he rubbed his mouth. "Probably since I last did it with you."

"Oh." She couldn't tear her gaze from his

fingers running softly over his lips. She knew they were as soft as they looked. She knew his taste. "You still scoffed."

He laughed. He actually laughed. Joy lit his face, his dark eyes warm.

Swallowing, she glanced away. It was too much. He made her feel too much. It was as if the emotion of eleven years that had been crammed inside her was expelling itself all at once.

Shaking his head, still smiling, he said, "So why do you hunt ghosts?"

Drawing in her breath, she pulled herself together. "I am a spiritualist and psychical phenomena inquiry agent."

"So…you hunt ghosts."

Opening her mouth to dispute him, she realised the folly in such an action. "I hunt ghosts," she reluctantly admitted.

"Have you found one?"

"Not as yet." She put her notebook in her pocket. "We should examine the next room."

He nodded, standing aside to allow her to lead them through the door to the earl's dressing room. "When did you start doing this?"

The earl's dressing room was much smaller than the bedchamber. "Always."

"Why do I not recall?

"You don't recall much."

A smile flirted with his lips. "Touché."

The window was much smaller also, letting in only a portion of the weak light from the bedchamber. Where was the lamp? Perhaps it was still in the earl's chamber. They should retrieve it to assist with the examination of the room.

"You were always odd."

Disturbed from her thoughts, she asked distractedly, "Pardon?"

A small smile played about his mouth. "You were always odd."

Blinking, she glanced away. It didn't hurt he thought so. She was odd. It was universally acknowledged. It didn't hurt.

"We used to sail ships in the conservatory," she said suddenly.

Now it was his turn to be confused. "What?"

The memory popped into her head, holding whatever this...feeling was at bay. "When it flooded. We used to sail ships. We would pretend to be captains of rival countries and the warfare in which we would engage was the stuff of legends. Or, at least, we thought so."

He studied her a moment. "Was your ship always green?" he asked finally.

"It is my favourite colour," she defended.

"I know, you always—" He stopped abruptly. Just as she was beginning to wonder why, he continued softly, "You always picked green."

Always. He had remembered she always picked green. Ducking her head, she resolved not to draw attention to his recollection unless he did. She would not push.

A quiet fell for some time as she moved

around the room.

"You have discounted the possibility of the moon flashing off the windows?" he said.

"I have not yet discounted it," she said. "It would be hard to establish at present, with the rain such as it is." She glanced at him. "I have also considered the possibility it could be you, lurking and such."

"Lurking?" His lips twitched.

She nodded. "And hulking. You have gotten extraordinarily large, you know."

An almost-smile playing about his mouth, he shrugged, those large muscles moving distractingly under the thin fabric of his shirt. "I cannot help it."

"You can help your muscles. Your brothers are not so large."

"Are we really discussing my physique when we could instead be investigating?"

"You are right." Squaring her shoulders, she got to work and ignored how his deliciously hulking presence made her breathless.

Chapter Six

THE WORDS ON THE page swam before him. Frowning, Maxim concentrated on making them still but they, stubborn bastards, changed order and shape, becoming nonsense. Most days, he could muddle through, but tonight he was tired and irritable, and that always made it worse.

Exhaling, he rubbed his eyes. He loved reading, he truly did, but it was always a struggle. What took others a moment took him four, and he knew it made him bothersome and slow. The pile of books on the table beside him was a challenge, but he *would* read every single one, even though he remembered his father sighing and directing him to more physical pursuits, even though his masters in America had cuffed him across the head whenever he'd had trouble reading their missives. Even though he wore the scars of those displeased with his doltishness on his skin and on his soul.

Now, though, he had a whole library of

books and no one to pester him. Well, no one but Alexandra. She sat in the chair opposite, her legs drawn up beneath her, frowning at her notebook as she pressed her pencil against her lips.

A flash of memory hit him, a younger Alexandra doing the same as they contemplated how best to explain to their respective parents the landslide wasn't really their fault and there was no way anyone could have a) predicted it and b) prevented it.

The shaft of the pencil dug deeper into the fullness of her bottom lip. He drew in his breath, his body hardening as he thought of other things he could press against those soft lips.

Damnation. Closing his eyes, he rubbed his brow. He shouldn't think such things, and especially not about her. He was a pent up mess of emotions, too cowardly to leave this hall and face his family. She deserved better than him.

Exhaling, he grabbed the cricket ball he'd placed on the table. He'd spied it in the nursery and something about it called to him, so he'd stolen it. It had felt familiar in his hand, the hard, shiny surface a comfort, his forefinger rubbing the raised seams. With a flick of his wrist, he flipped the ball in the air, caught it, flipped again. And again. And again.

Across the room, Alexandra's frown increased.

She'd always been studious. When they were younger, she'd carried around notebooks, jotting down thoughts and observations. He'd stolen the notebooks, but the words had swum before him and so he'd drawn in them, little scribbles to make her smile. It had always awed him, that she was so clever.

All day they'd traipsed through the upper reaches of the house, she cataloguing and he holding her equipment. It should have been tedious, but he was beginning to believe nothing could be tedious with her. His life since he'd woken in America had been work—first as a servant in his rescuer's home and then as a longshoreman and, finally, as a sailor. He'd had little of ease and contentment, and he'd had no time to pursue an interest simply because one was interested, and certainly not one as strange as ghost hunting.

She'd always been odd, but he admired that about her. She was unconcerned with the expectation of others, and her parents had loved her, her siblings had looked up to her, and he...he'd loved her too. She'd been his best friend, his partner in crime, the person he turned to when he'd needed comfort.

Maxim flicked his wrist. The ball spun in the air, flipping over itself, and he knew if he threw it, the ball would spin wildly and take the batsman unaware.... A memory, clear as day, of his brother stood at the crease, swinging wildly at the ball hurtling to him. Spinning around, Stephen had landed on his arse and Maxim had doubled over with laughter while Stephen used every curse they'd ever heard the groundskeepers use.

The ball made a dull smack as it landed in his palm. This place drew memories from him, and if he were honest with himself, so did she. Alexandra. It was as if a piece of him had been missing, and she fitted him perfectly. He was content in her presence, calmer, the ragged pieces of him soothed. God damn, but he lo—

He threw the ball above him. Hard. He hadn't thought that. Hadn't even considered it. Almost two nights she'd been here, and it was beginning to be that he couldn't imagine a time when she was not, but he didn't—he couldn't— He was too broken, too dull-witted.

He'd misstepped, badly, when he'd kissed her. In some mangled part of his brain, he'd thought the warning warranted but it wasn't until he'd had her under him, his arm about her waist and her soft lips on his, that he'd realised how horribly mistaken he'd been. It had never been about a lesson.

Sighing, she stretched her neck. He almost dropped the ball. Would that same look be on her face as he traced the cord of her neck with his tongue, his hand covering her breast as she squirmed and moaned....

Viciously, he flipped the ball, catching it as it careened wildly back to him, flipped, caught, flipped, caught, and he willed his body to behave.

Focussing again on the notebook, Alexandra wrote down something.

Snatching the ball, he rolled it between his

hands. "Surely now would be a good time to investigate?"

"Hmm?" Alexandra said, still regarding her notebook.

"Now would be a good time to investigate." He waved a hand at the window. "It is dark, after all."

She glanced up distractedly. "I have not yet finished with my preliminary investigations and those must be completed first."

"Why?" Restlessness beat at him. He wanted to be away from this room, wanted to be occupied, so he wasn't staring at her and imagining the taste of her against his tongue.

"Because my findings will be tainted if I do not. Stop interrupting me." She frowned at the page. "I've written the same thing three times."

Pushing himself to his feet, he said, "Maybe I will investigate on my own."

"You will taint my results," she said, still looking at her notebook.

"No, I won't. I'll be helping."

"You really won't."

He made to take a step. "I'm going now."

Before he'd realised what had happened, she'd propelled herself from her chair and shoved him, right in the centre of his chest. Surprised, he fell, landing hard on his arse as she clambered over him, pushing his shoulders to the floor.

Then, she sat on his chest.

"You're sitting on me," he said incredulously.

"You're not going anywhere," she stated, the familiar stubborn cast to her chin.

"You're *sitting* on me. I'm twice the size of you."

Hands bearing down on his shoulders, she said, "It always stopped you before."

"I'm *twice* the size of you." This may have worked when they were fourteen and fifteen, but he'd grown a foot and had muscle to match. It was a simple matter to flip her over. She squawked, struggling to rise as he straddled her and pinned her arms to the ground.

"Get off me," she demanded

"Things are different now," he crowed.

"Maxim, get off!"

"No." He grinned down at her.

Scowling, she tried to buck him off, but he easily subdued such pitiful efforts. Giving up, she glared at him, her chest heaving.

Her hips were trapped between his thighs. Her fingers curled, brushing the back of his hands that held her wrists. She was so soft beneath him.

Breathing suddenly became difficult and he tensed, his body hardening as he stared down at her, his gaze drifting to her mouth. She watched him with big eyes, her lips parted as she drew quick breath, her tongue flicking out to leave wetness behind. Stifling a groan, he shifted to hold himself from her and hoped like hell she couldn't feel his hard length against her.

Letting her go, he backed away from her. "I'm twice the size of you," he said, voice full of gravel.

Slowly, she rose to a seated position, her gaze never leaving him.

His groin ached, his skin felt too small for his body, and he wanted so badly to kiss her. "Stop staring at me," he growled.

She didn't.

"Alexandra!"

She blinked. Desire melted from her expression. "That is the first time you've used my name."

That couldn't be right. "Really?"

She nodded and then, averting her eyes, she sniffed.

"You're not going to cry, are you?" he asked suspiciously.

Biting her lip, she shook her head.

"Don't be a girl." Her chin wobbled. "Alexandra." Tears spilled over. "Ah, hell." Awkwardly, he enfolded her in his arms.

Her head nestled into his shoulder. It felt...right. Resting his check against her hair, he closed his eyes. Was it only two days ago she'd appeared back in his life?

Against him, she took a deep breath. "There's nothing wrong with being a girl." The words were muffled against his chest.

"Beg yours?"

She pushed away. Wet hazel eyes regarded him steadily. "There's nothing wrong with being a girl. You said it like it was an insult. It's not an insult, Maxim."

"I—No. Sorry."

Nodding, she moved away from him. He wanted to haul her back to him, to feel her breath against his skin, her softness against him.

Abruptly, memories crashed upon him. Harsh shouting. A closed fist against his cheek. A hard hand cuffing the back of his head. The bite of a whip.

"Maxim?"

He didn't look up. If he did, she would read his every thought.

Gentle fingers stroked his forearm. "Maxim?"

Her hand. Small, but so capable. When she wrote, the letters she formed were precise and graceful, a work of art on the page. Nothing like the mess he made. He saw again the face of the bosun, the spittle flying as he screamed. "Tell me of your ghost."

Her fingers stilled. "Where did you go?"

Shaking his head, he said, "It doesn't matter."

"Maxim—"

"It doesn't. Tell me a ghost story, Alexandra."

Just when he thought he was going to have to press her again, she sighed softly. "Which one?"

"The one you think currently haunts Waithe Hall."

"There are many stories."

"But only one has captured your interest."

Settling beside him, she folded her hands in her lap. "Margaret Howard. She was the housekeeper here in the early 1700s."

"Margaret Howard." He turned the name over in his mind. "I don't remember her tale."

Lips quirking, she raised her brows.

He smiled ruefully. "Haha, yes, I know. I don't remember much, et cetera and so forth."

Still smirking, she continued. "The earl at the time sympathised with the Jacobite rebellion and opened his home to the rebels, hiding them from crown forces. Margaret Howard liked her cups too well and one night, she liked them with the wrong people. She was free with her words, and the local garrison learned of the earl's leanings."

"I gather they weren't words the earl wanted the garrison to hear."

"Far from it. They stormed Waithe Hall, but they found nothing."

"Nothing? Ah. The secret passages."

She nodded. "But Margaret Howard had been careless. When it came time to lock the house, she could not find her keys. At the time she thought little of it, certain they would return when she least expected it.

"One night, the garrison stole into Waithe Hall and slaughtered the rebels. There was no sign of forced entry, and whispers began that Margaret Howard sympathised with the crown, that she'd opened the door for them, that she'd given them her keys."

Drawing her knees up, she said, "She protested her innocence, but none believed her. She searched and searched, but she could not find them. She became frantic. She had failed the earl once. She could not fail him again. One night, she searched on the parapet, and...." She paused dramatically. "She slipped. The next morning, they found her body. She was given a pauper's funeral, but it wasn't long before odd happenings began. It could be the wind, or the glow of the moon, but some...some say she searches still."

A smile tugged at him. Alexandra glowed, her passion obvious. "I remember that story. I didn't know it was about Margaret Howard, though."

"It was always the best one," she said. "Do you remember Timmons used to tell them to us, and you were always scared?"

"I was never *scared*," he said. "I was simply impatient to start riding. Timmons *was* our groom."

"You were scared."

"*Maybe* I was nervous."

"No, you were scared. I—Ah!" He tickled her and she dissolved into giggles, half-heartedly fending off his attack. A grin tugged at his lips, and the strangeness of carefree joy rushed through him.

Eventually, they calmed, lying on their sides next to each other. He studied her face so close to his. The shape of her brow, the colour of her eyes, the curve of her jaw, the way she tucked her hand beneath her chin. He committed all to his memory, such that he would never forget her again.

Her eyes drifted shut, and he, content to be by her side, fell asleep as well.

Chapter Seven

HEAD AGAINST THE WALL, Maxim sat beside her, arm braced over one drawn up leg. Again he wore only a shirt, the neck open and baring a strong neck and jaw. In profile, his lashes hid the warm brown of his half-closed eyes, and dark stubble covered his jaw.

She was staring at him again. Jerking her gaze away, Alexandra looked down at the notebook in her lap. They'd been in the earl's chamber since night had fallen after a day spent examining room after room, and as yet no spiritual activity had made itself known. She was not hopeful. Nothing of her investigations suggested the presence of a spirit. More likely any lights had been Maxim himself, or perhaps the villagers had been mistaken.

Her gaze drifted back to him. She couldn't remember him ever before being so still. When they were children, he'd constantly been in motion, unable to sit for more than a few moments.

He swallowed, the movement of his throat mesmerising. Forcing her gaze from him once more, she examined instead the room. The mother-of-pearl inlaid in the mantelpiece glowed in the lamplight, casting a soft haze through the room that was reflected in the over-large, bevel-edged mirror—

Her shoulders drooped. "Oh."

Maxim glanced at her, his eyes shadowed in the light. "What is it?"

"Look." Getting to her feet, she brought the lamp near the fireplace. The mother of pearl glowed, caught by the mirror which amplified the light. "The cover has fallen off the mirror. The moon probably shone through the window, bounced off the inlay and reflected in the window."

"So it is solved?"

Disappointment licking through her, she stared at the mirror. "I think so."

"But you are not certain."

"As certain as I can be."

"After less than four hours in this room, you have solved the case?"

The mockery in his tone took her by surprise. "I am good at this, Maxim."

Picking at the fabric covering his knee, he didn't respond. Finally, he said, "So, will you leave?"

She didn't want to. "It still rains."

"And that is why you will stay?"

It wasn't her only reason. She would stay because of him. She would stay because it hurt to think of being where he wasn't.

A thought occurred. "I think we should try to find the keys." She warmed to the idea. "We should start tonight."

Maxim got to his feet and held out his hand. "Come on, then."

He hadn't even hesitated. He hadn't protested it a ridiculous notion. He'd merely offered his assistance. Swallowing against the lump in her throat, she placed her hand in his.

"Your hair." He pushed a lock of her hair behind her ear, his fingers tracing the shell.

Breath caught, she stared up at him.

Intensely, he watched his thumb as it dragged across her jaw. Meeting her eyes, he cleared his throat. "I'll take the lamp, shall I?"

Dazed, she nodded. Collecting the lamp, he opened the door, strangely hesitant as he departed the chamber. Shaking herself, she followed.

Maxim led the way, holding the lamp high as they traversed the hallway. Alexandra trained her gaze on his broad back. He *had* changed from the Maxim she remembered, but so much was the same. He may be rougher, and perhaps a bit gruff, but he was still her Maxim. He was still the boy who was her best friend. He was still the boy she loved.

"Where do you want to start?" He turned, the lamp throwing light across his body. "Which room?"

Taking a breath, she focussed on the task at hand. "Maybe the housekeeper's room? The one on this level?"

"Maybe? Or we should?"

"We should."

"Right." He started toward the servant's quarters.

"Maxim?"

He stopped. "Yes?"

"Why are you helping me?"

He frowned. "Why wouldn't I?"

Biting her lip, she forced herself to ask, "Do you think me odd?"

The corner of his lips turned up. "Of course. Did I not say so already?"

He had. He had said she was odd and it hadn't hurt, just as it didn't now. Everyone thought her odd. She told this to herself so often, it had to be true.

"But you are Alexandra," he continued.

"What? What does that mean? That doesn't mean anything."

"Yes, it does. You are magnificently odd. You are yourself, wholly and utterly. I have never met someone so unapologetically themselves. And you want to *help*. We're traipsing about this house because you wish to help a ghost. A *ghost*, Alexandra." A grin flashed across his face. "You were always such fun."

"Oh." A little kernel of warmth burned inside her. He thought her *magnificently* odd.

With another little smile, he turned and

continued down the hall.

She started to follow only to stop as something caught her eye. "Maxim, wait a moment."

He kept on, taking the light with him.

Darkness rushed to fill the hall, but there was enough light for her to approach one of the doors. There was something…. She wasn't sure what, but they should….

"Maxim," she called again, unable to take her eyes from the door.

"What?" he said, right next to her ear.

She jumped about a foot. "Don't scare me like that! What did you do with the lamp?"

"You're the one who stopped." Striding ahead, he picked up the lamp he'd clearly left for the express purpose of startling her. Returning to her, he lifted the lamp higher. "What is it?"

The light cast against a perfectly ordinary door. "I don't know. There's something about this door."

"The door or the room?" He reached for the doorknob.

"No, Maxim, do not—" The door opened. She cringed. Nothing rushed at them from the darkness.

He made as if to enter.

"Maxim, what if—"

Shooting her an impatient look, he said, "What? The ghost might get me?"

She sniffed. "She might."

Lifting the lamp high, he looked about the

room. "See. No ghost. Come on." He disappeared inside.

Cautiously, she followed. The light fell upon a large bedchamber, with the bed itself set into a nook cut into the wall, curtains framing the opening. Like the rest of Waithe Hall, holland covers draped furniture that seemed to be a chaise longue, a desk and chair, a dresser and a chest of drawers. The bed itself still had the mattress and its hangings, while the balcony doors were reflected in a huge mirror opposite.

Maxim stood in the room's centre as, brow knitted, he stared at the bed. "This is where Queen Anne stayed when she visited Waithe Hall."

"Really?"

"I remember my father telling me that, quite proudly. I remember, Alexandra." Striding through the room, he tore a cover off to reveal a lacquered writing desk. "This was a purchase by my great-grandfather, who brought it back from the continent." He gestured to the mirror. "That came from Venice, and was commissioned by the fifth earl."

A bemused smile tugged at her. "I did not know you knew the history so well."

"Nor did I." Running his hand over the mantle, he glanced at her. "What made you stop here?"

She sighed. "I don't know. There is no spirit, and no reports this room was ever visited by one."

"Well, there's nothing here." The corner of his mouth lifted. "Or maybe.... There is a ghost."

"Pardon?"

"Perhaps *I* am the ghost."

Rolling her eyes, she said, "Do not be foolish."

Eyes alight, he made a ghostly noise as he rushed toward her.

"Maxim." Hugging herself, she bowed her head. "Don't tease."

"I'm not, Alexandra." Finger raising her chin, his gaze searched hers. "I'm not."

Taking a breath, she nodded.

"Are you often teased?"

"Not often." At least, not anymore. "Besides, I do not care for the opinions of others." And she did not. Not anymore. Not much.

"But you care for mine."

She nodded, even though he hadn't asked a question. "Of course. You know that."

A strange look crossed his features. "I do," he said slowly.

They stared at each other. His scent wound about her, woodsy and spice, and she wanted...she wanted to touch him. She wanted to trace the planes of his face, feel the softness of his sulky lips, the rasp of his beard. She wanted to trace the muscles of his chest, his stomach, wanted to dig her hands into his back as he touched her. He was so beautiful, this boy she once knew.

"Alexandra," he said in the hush.

Her gaze fell to his lips. "Yes?"

"I'm going to kiss you."

Her eyes drifted shut. "Yes."

Their lips met. It was soft, sweet, tentative, and he made her feel safe and, made her feel...beloved.

Hand rising to cup her cheek, he traced the seam of her lips with his tongue. Tangling her hands in his hair, she opened, gasping as he invaded her mouth. Groaning, he kissed her harder, kissed her again, his hand pressing into the small of her back to drag her closer. She'd imagined this, more often than she should. As a girl, she couldn't count the times she'd stared at him and wished his mouth on hers.

Trailing kisses over her cheek, her jaw, the cord of her neck, his hand drifted down her throat. She gripped the hard, round muscle of his shoulders, her fingers digging into his flesh as she arched into his touch. Hard fingers whispered against her breast, and then covered it.

She sucked in her breath.

He stilled, his lips brushing her neck. "What am I doing?" he murmured, breath hot against her skin. "I am taking what is not mine."

She tugged on his hair. He raised his head but he wouldn't meet her eyes. "You take nothing. I'm giving myself to you, as you give yourself to me."

Dark eyes met hers. "And what of your future husband?"

"What of your future wife?" she countered.

A quick, rueful smile tugged at his lips. "Touché."

Brushing her lips over his jaw, she said, "There is only us, and only now."

Cupping her face, he feathered his thumbs over her temples. "You are odd."

The affection in his tone took the sting from the words. "I know."

Sobering, he met her eyes. "Are you certain?"

She traced his brow, the curve of his ear. "It's always been you, Maxim."

His gaze heated. "It's always been you, Alexandra."

They crashed into each other. She moaned as his lips forced hers open, their tongues duelling. He backed her into the bed and she fell onto the sheets. He placed a knee on the edge of the mattress, looming over her before he took her mouth again.

The pins and ties of her gown and stays gave easily under their eager fingers. He tugged at his shirt and she helped him pull it over his head, revealing heavy pectorals, a flat stomach ridged with muscle, and—

She drew in her breath.

A thin scar curled around his hip, licking up to his belly button. Tentatively, she raised her hand. He flinched when she touched him. "What happened?" she asked softly.

"I didn't pay attention."

His shoulder bore another. "And here?"

"I was too uppity."

There was another, thinner scar near his hairline at the temple.

He closed his eyes. "That was from the wreck."

Leaning forward, she cupped his chin as she placed her lips against the scar at his temple, following its line with gentle kisses.

A groan burst from him and he hauled her into his lap, her legs sprawling either side of his hips, his hands braced against her back. He took her mouth, demanding entrance, and she granted it, wrapping her arms about his neck as they devoured each other.

"Maxim?"

He nuzzled her neck. "Hmm?"

"I haven't done this before."

He lifted his head. She drowned in dark eyes before his lashes lowered. "I haven't either."

"Really?"

He gave a sharp nod.

She placed her hand against his cheek. Reluctantly, he met her gaze. She smiled softly, and kissed him. His arms tightened about her as he kissed her back.

His hand covered her breast, her nipple tight against his palm as he shaped her flesh. Tearing herself from his lips, she arched as she wound her arms about his shoulders. His lips trailed down her neck, her chest, and then he covered her nipple with his mouth. Moaning, she pushed herself into him, feeling him hard and hot between her thighs. Desire flooded her, and she felt so empty.

He made a choked sound and suddenly she was on her back, her thighs hugging his hips as his hands planted either side of her head, holding him above her. He pushed himself against her, deep thrusts that drove her wild. Reaching down, she opened his breeches, her fingers meeting the flesh of his flank. Her chemise was rucked up around her stomach, and she gasped as the hardness of him pressed against her with no barrier.

Stilling, he held himself above her. "Are you sure?"

Running her hands over his buttocks, she made a noise of impatience. "Are *you* sure?"

His brows shot up.

"You're the one who keeps asking," she said.

"I'm being considerate."

"You're being annoying.

Shaking his head, he said, "I can't believe we're arguing *now*."

Her lips twitched. "We are odd, aren't we?"

Returning her smile, he touched her forehead with his. "We are."

Holding his breath, he moved. The broad head of him pressed against her. Biting her lip, she held his gaze.

He shuddered. "You feel so good, Alexandra."

It started to burn a little, but he was slow and cautious and she wanted it so much.

He froze. "I am hurting you."

"It always hurts. Just get it over with."

"Get it over with?"

"You know what I mean."

Braced over her, he hung his head. "We are arguing. Again."

"Come inside me, Maxim," she whispered.

His eyes darkened with lust, and he pushed. She drew in her breath, the burn turning to pain. Forehead against hers, he nudged again, and then he was inside her.

Wonder filled her. Maxim was inside her.

Chest heaving, he stilled. The burn began to recede and she moved experimentally.

He made a choked sound. "Christ. Don't move."

"Why?" It felt good if she moved just so.

"Don't. I won't be able to—" His hands tightened to fists beside her head.

Pleasure began to spiral through her again. She moaned. "Maxim."

He exploded into motion. His hips thrust against her, forcing him into her again and again. Her neck arched, pleasure pumping through her as he moved over her, as they found a rhythm that wrecked them both.

"Alexandra," he groaned, his hands gripping her thighs, dragging her into his thrusts. The different angle rubbed him against a spot inside her that made sensation bloom, bright and blinding, and she shattered into a million pieces.

He cursed and moaned and then he joined her, finding his own release.

Breath harsh, she came back to herself slowly. He was heavy atop her, his face buried in her neck, his body shaking.

Stroking his back, she whispered, "It was always you."

Raising his head, he met her gaze. Wrapping her in his arms, he kissed her temple and whispered back, "It was always you."

Chapter Eight

Rain battered the window as early morning light fell in a weak shaft upon the bed, outlining the shape of their legs beneath the rumpled covers. Alexandra lay curled beside him, her hand beneath her cheek. A blonde curl rested on her bare shoulder, her skin creamy and soft. He'd kissed her there, and followed a path to her breasts, hidden by the sheet covering them both.

She looked so peaceful. He would be a cad to disturb her while she slept.

"I can feel you looking at me," she said, her eyes remaining closed.

Maxim shifted. He was half-hard, and it wouldn't take much to bring him the rest of the way. "You are amazingly fascinating," he said.

She cracked one eye. "What a Banbury tale."

"It's not my fault you do not understand how fascinating you are."

Putting the back of her hand to her temple,

she shielded her eyes. "Don't try turning it up."

Pulling her hand from her eyes, he said, "You. Are. Fascinating."

A tiny smile played about her lips. "If you say so."

"I do." Unable to help himself, he traced her brow with his thumb. Eyes darkening, she shivered under his touch. He grinned wolfishly, obscenely proud he could make her react so. "When did you start liking the occult?"

"I've always liked it," she responded, her voice husky.

"No, you didn't."

Clearing her throat, she rolled her eyes. "Why do you think I always wanted to investigate the attic, and the smugglers caves, and the ruins?"

"Because we were children and it was fun?"

"Well, yes, but it was also because ghosts are fascinating."

"Why?" Goosebumps met his fingers as he stroked again, and again.

"They still have work on this earth. They linger, because something remains unfinished, or their anger, their grief, their love, some emotion is so great, so terrible, that not even death can fully claim them."

A smile tugged at him. "You are a romantic."

"What? No."

"You are."

Her gaze drifted past him. "You know, I

think I might be," she finally said.

"So now you investigate Waithe Hall."

"Yes. There was always strange things occurring, even before you returned." She fell silent a moment. "Where were you, Maxim?"

What to say? "As near as I can tell, my ship wrecked somewhere in the Atlantic. I was discovered by sailors and brought to Boston. I could not recall who I was, so they patched me up and sent me on my way. After a time, I recalled more of my life before, and made my way to London, where I recalled even more and I made my way to Waithe Hall—"

"What a load of codswallop," she interrupted calmly.

His mouth fell open in shock. "What?" he finally managed.

"That is a fine story, and perhaps it is even true, but you're not telling me everything."

How did she know? How— But then, this was Alexandra. She once knew everything of him, just as he knew everything of her.

"What else happened?"

He shook his head, his thoughts muddled, and he didn't want to tell her, he didn't want to admit—

Careful fingers glided over the scar at his shoulder. "Then tell me of this. How did this happen?"

"A woman took me in, out of the goodness of her Christian heart, and gave me room and board in return for service. I did not move fast enough for her liking one day." He felt detached from the recollection, as if it were someone else's tale he told.

Biting her upper lip, she touched the smooth patch of skin on his left side. "And this?"

"Scalding water. I worked in a laundry after the Christian woman turned me out."

The scar bisecting his chest. "And this?"

"The rope I was using to haul freight in the docks slipped."

Following the movement of her touch with her eyes, she said, "No one thought to question your accent? Your manner?"

"They tried to beat it from me. Said I was putting on airs."

"And you didn't remember."

Phantom pain, such as when one of his employers cuffed him, feathered across his cheekbone. He rubbed at it. "I still do not remember everything, but I remembered enough to know England was home. I obtained employment on a ship bound for Portsmouth, thinking if I returned to London I would remember more."

"When was that?"

He stared at her hand. Her fingers were slender, the nails bitten. She always had bitten her nails. "Two years ago."

Her hand jerked. "Pardon?"

Keeping his eyes on her hand, he said, "I half-remembered who I was, where I was from. I thought living in London would help."

"You have been in England for two years?" she said, an edge to her tone.

"I *did not* remember. Not until—" Frustration hardened his jaw. Christ, why did he want to tell her *everything*?

"Until?"

He exhaled in defeat. "Not until I saw Oliver."

"Your brother? The *earl*?"

He winced at her tone. "Oliver—I suppose he's Roxwaithe now—he was seated in the earl's carriage, and it was pure luck he drew the curtains aside to look out to the street. The crest had been newly painted—probably because he was the new earl—and I looked at it, I looked at *him*, and I knew. I knew who he was. It was the first time I had looked at someone and could recall them from before." A million images had barraged him all at once, and the one that had crystallised the most had been Waithe Hall...and the girl with the golden hair.

Turning on his back, he stared unseeingly at the bed canopy. "He was gone before I could approach, and that perhaps was for the best. I gathered what few belongings I had and made my way to Waithe Hall. To home. I did not know it was shuttered, that Oliver—Roxwaithe—and Stephen no longer resided here. I had nowhere to go, so I made it my home."

"Nowhere to go? Nowhere—" She took a breath. "How long have you been at Waithe Hall?"

"Five months."

Her eyes glittered. "So instead of finding us, of telling us you were alive, instead you let us continue to believe you dead and you came instead here? Do I have the right of it?"

"I couldn't," he burst out. "I just...couldn't, Alexandra." He balled his hands to fists. She didn't understand. She couldn't, because she didn't know everything. She didn't know what had sent him from England to begin with.

"I fought with my father before I left, did you know? He—I—" He closed his eyes. He was going to have to tell her. "I was sent down from Eton. For cheating."

Silence stretched between them.

"I cannot read. Not well. The words become jumbled, and I cannot—" He punched his thigh. "I have never been good at reading and writing. You know this."

"It doesn't matter—" she said.

"It does!" A hundred taunts, a thousand, tumbled through his mind. The boys at Eton. His employers in America. His brothers. His *father*. "It *does* matter. I could not complete my studies. I had to *pay* someone to do it for me. The master caught us, and they said I cheated, and I suppose by their reckoning I did, but it was my work, Alexandra. It was mine."

Gaze trained on the bed canopy, he saw again his father before him. "I had never seen my father so...cold. Always before, his anger would run hot—you remember, do you not? —but once his disappointment was expressed, he would say how the wrong could be righted, which lesson could be learned, and all was forgiven."

Fingers tightening in the sheets, he saw again his father before him, his face stripped of expression. "That day, though, that day he was calm. Eerily calm. He asked me if it was true. I could not lie. I *had* paid another boy to write my essays for me. I could not deny it. He—"

He swallowed. The look on his father's face.... It had made him feel small and panicked, and he, idiot child that he had been, had responded with fury. "I yelled, and I threatened, and I told him it was his fault I was stupid, his fault that I couldn't keep up with the studies, that the words swam on the page before me. It was because of him I'd had to pay that boy to help me, and he should have known better. Why had he insisted on sending me to Eton, when we both knew I was a dolt who would have done better as a ship-hand on one of the Waithe ships. I threatened to leave on one of those ships. He told me if I left, I shouldn't bother to return." Bitterness soured his mouth. "I left."

She said nothing but he could feel her eyes upon him. "I was a stupid fifteen-year-old child who threw his life away after a fight with his father. And now I'll never see my father again, he'll never know—" He could never apologise. His father had gone to his grave without knowing how sorry his son was that they'd fought, that his stupidity had brought them this mess.

For a long time, she was silent. "That is unfortunate."

Giving a hiccoughing laugh, he dug the heels of his hands into his eyes. She said it so matter-of-factly, as if he hadn't just told her his worst secret.

"Maxim?"

Still unable to speak, he shook his head. Only Alexandra.

She pulled his hands away and narrowed hazel eyes met his. "What is it?"

"The great tragedy of my life and you've reduced it to, 'That is unfortunate.'"

Her frown deepened. "Well, it is unfortunate. It is unfortunate we thought you dead. It is unfortunate you fought with your father. It is unfortunate your body is riddled with scars, that I was without you for eleven years. All of it. It is all unfortunate." Still holding his hands, she looked him direct. "You know your father loved you."

Ducking his head, he stared at her shoulder.

"Maxim." She tugged at his hands. "He loved you."

He smiled bitterly. "We'll never know."

"*I* know. We mourned, Maxim. Your father, your brothers. I did not know of your argument, but you can be sure he felt the lack of you."

"You cannot be sure."

"Do you believe our families ceased our acquaintance with your disappearance? If anything, it brought us closer. Your father had need of mine, and as his closest friend, my father was only too happy to provide whatever he could. Until the day he died, your father loved and missed you. You can be certain." She threaded her fingers through the hair at his temple. "Your brothers would want to see you."

"I'm not ready to see them."

"We are never ready to do the things that frighten us, but you are alive, Maxim. You deserve to take your place amongst your family."

"I am not ready, Alexandra."

She sighed. "Fine. But know I shall not give up on this."

A smile touched his lips through all the bitterness. She was always so determined. "I shouldn't presume you would." He ran his thumb over her mouth. "I remembered you."

Her lips parted under his touch. "Pardon?"

"I didn't remember your name, but I remembered you. I never forgot, Alexandra." Her skin glowed. Her hair was a golden halo around her face. He wanted her so much.

Lust punched him. Flipping her over, he settled between her thighs. "Are you sore?" he asked thickly.

An answering lust rose in her eyes. "No."

"Good." He covered her mouth with his and neither of them talked for a long, long time.

Chapter Nine

ALEXANDRA STOOD BEFORE THE
window, sunlight from the curtain she held open
surrounding her in a golden haze that outlined the
shape of her body beneath her chemise.

A foolish grin stretching his features,
Maxim pushed himself up from the bed. She
looked so beautiful, her hair in a riotous tangle
down her back, the skin he'd kissed and caressed
creamy in the sunlight. At some point, they'd
made their way back to the chamber he'd made
his. He'd never before shared his bed with
someone, but it seemed natural to have her by his
side. For a day and a half, they'd only left the
chamber for food, and it had been the best damn
day and a half of his life.

The sheet pooled around his lap, leaving his
chest bare. Should he cover himself? But then,
she'd kissed and caressed every part of him as
well.

"Alexandra?" She turned. The light had

turned her chemise partly transparent and he could see the shape of her breast, the pink flesh of her nipple. Lust stirred, hardening him. "What are you doing?" he said, and wondered how soon he could have her in bed beside him.

"The rain has stopped," she said.

His lust died and panic rose to take its place. There was nothing to keep her here. Her ghost was not a ghost. The rain had stopped. She could leave.

They stared at each other.

"What are you going to do?" he finally asked.

She wrapped her arms about herself. "Search for the keys." She sounded hesitant, and she looked at him warily, as if she expected him to argue with her, to claim she should return home. That she should leave him.

She couldn't be more wrong. Fierce joy tore through him and, shoving the covers aside, he vaulted from the bed. She squeaked when he took her in his arms, the sound changing to a moan when he covered her lips with his. Heat and lust and need rioted in his blood as he lifted her against him, as she wrapped her legs about his waist, as he drowned himself in her taste.

She tore her mouth from his. "Are you that excited by the search for Margaret Howard's keys?" she said breathlessly.

"What?" he mumbled, licking the cord of her neck. Holding her thighs, he stepped forward until the wall met her back.

Fingers tightening in his hair, she arched as he made small thrusts between her thighs, her chemise and his drawers the only thing separating them. "You seem to have reacted favourably to my suggestion we search for her keys."

"Oh. Yes. Her keys." She tasted like salt and cream at the juncture of her neck and, when he took the soft flesh of the lobe of her ear between his teeth, it made her gasp.

"Maxim, we should—should start to—oh, goodness, what are you—Maxim?"

"Hmm?"

"We…should…." She trailed off.

Taking her chemise in his hand, he drew it upwards. "We should?"

"Never mind," she said, and dragged his mouth back to hers.

***

"YOU CAN SEE THE road from this room."

Alexandra looked up from her notebook. "Hmm?"

"This window," Maxim said. "You can see it from the road."

"Which one?" she asked, still composing the note she wanted to write in her head.

"The only road. The one to Waithe Village. Are you paying attention?"

"Yes, of course." She needed to record the actions they had already taken. They'd, unfortunately, debunked the presence of a ghost, or at least a presence in the room the villagers had reported as containing activity. Perhaps Margaret Howard did roam these halls, and perhaps finding her keys would help her find peace, but if Alexandra were being honest, she was prolonging her investigation solely to spend more time with Maxim.

"You're not listening to me," the man himself said in her ear.

She braced a hand against her wildly beating heart. "Damnation, Maxim, don't *do* that." He had a *horrible* penchant for startling her.

He just grinned and went back to the window, propping a foot on the seat set into the alcove. He again wore only shirt and breeches, and she ran her gaze over his form, remembering how he looked out of them….

Clearing her throat, she returned to her notes. He so easily distracted her. He would brush her hair back into place, and she would lose all train of thought. When they walked the hallways, he would take her hand to lace her fingers with his and she would forget where they were going. Or he would simply stand as he was now, and she became breathless.

This was her fifth day at Waithe Hall. How could so much change in five days?

Forcing herself to concentrate, she said, "I think we should revisit the housekeeper's room."

"Which one?" he asked, removing his foot from the seat to fold his arms before his chest.

The move pulled the fabric of his shirt tight, and she remembered the feel of that resilient muscle beneath her hands.

Focus, Alexandra. "The one on the first floor, not the ground floor." She frowned at her notes. "There is something strange about it."

Moving beside her, he looked over her shoulder at her notebook. "Strange how?"

A delicious thrill ran through her at his closeness. Giving in to it, she leaned into him, and he automatically brought her into his embrace, looping his arm around her. "The shape of it is odd."

Resting his chin on her shoulder, he said, "I'll take your word for it."

"You do not think it an odd shape?"

"I have no idea, but if you think it odd, then it must be."

So easily he accepted her. Swallowing the lump in her throat, she said, "So will you investigate with me?"

"Of course. I'd follow you anywhere." He planted a kiss against her neck. "Besides, following you is inevitably exciting. You always discover the best things."

Her chest tightened. "Right then, shall we?" she said briskly, ignoring the feelings he stirred so easily.

"We shall." Taking her hand, he led her from the room.

She snuck glances at him as they walked down the corridor past the open court. A faint smile lit his face, his expression easy. Was it only five days ago he'd scowled and growled at her?

Of a sudden, he stopped stock still. "We should go through the secret passage from the countess's chamber to the nursery," he announced.

She blinked. "What? Why?"

"Because it's fun," he said, eyes alight with glee.

"It takes longer," she pointed out.

"What else do we have to do?"

"True." Playing at reluctance, she protested as she allowed him to reverse their course and drag her to the countess's suite. They'd used this passage several times, and most of the dust and cobwebs had been swept away by their travels. Following behind him, she stepped over the debris that had accumulated over the years. The structures themselves were sound, which she supposed spoke well of the earls who had commissioned their construction—

Again, Maxim stopped suddenly, such that she crashed into his back. Whirling around, he pinned her against the wall.

"What are you d—" His mouth covered hers.

Opening, she allowed his lips to ravish hers. Lust and want and need arched between them, and she gripped his shoulders, wanting to kiss him forever.

Pulling back, he grinned. "I've always wanted to do that."

Pretending herself unaffected, she snorted. He laughed, flipping a lock of her hair, and they continued on.

The passage opened into the schoolroom, one of the suite of rooms dedicated to the nursery. Maxim's expression turned grim as they passed through, his deliberate gaze falling on anything but the small desks situated in the corner. She'd rarely been in this room, and never when the Roxwaithe children were undertaking lessons. She could only imagine what he recalled. Judging by his expression, it wasn't pleasant.

"Master Emery always used to call me imbecilic," he said suddenly.

What could she say to that? She remained silent, and hoped he would continue.

"He had a cane. A long, thin birch rod. It made a wicked loud sound when it struck his desk. The sound was duller when it hit flesh."

He had his back to her, broad and strong, but his shoulders were hunched, every muscle tense. Wrapping her arms around him, she rested her head on his shoulder blade, her hands laced over his abdomen.

His hand crept over hers. "He used to correct me the most. Oliver and Stephen were only occasionally the focus of his ire. I was foolish, you understand. I could not read a simple sentence without making an error, could not write legibly, no matter what correction he was forced to administer. He was always forced, you understand."

She tightened her grip. "You are not stupid, Maxim."

He, if possible, tensed further. "You said it."

"What? No. When?"

Moving from her, he turned, his gaze averted and his arms about himself. "That first night."

What? She hadn't— "Do you mean when we argued?"

He shrugged.

She stared at him in disbelief. "You cannot hold that against me. I did not know. Besides, you were *being* stupid. I would never say you *are* stupid."

He shrugged again.

"I did not mean—Maxim. I do not think you stupid."

"It doesn't matter."

"It *does*. You are not stupid." Framing his face with her hands, she glared. "You are not stupid."

They were locked like that for a time. Finally, the corner of his mouth lifted. "You can be quite fierce."

"You are not to think yourself stupid," she said intently.

"All right."

"I mean it."

"I believe you."

"Good."

For a long moment, they remained locked together. "We should make our way to the housekeeper's chamber," he finally said.

Taking a breath, she allowed her hands to fall. "Yes."

"Alexandra." Capturing her hand, he lifted it to his mouth. She shivered as he brushed her palm with his lips. "Thank you."

Those weren't tears burning her eyes. "You're welcome."

They left the schoolroom. It took some moments to reach the housekeeper's chamber, all passed in silence. Beyond the other servants' rooms, the housekeeper's was bare of most furnishing. A metal bedframe occupied one corner of the room, absent mattress, and a washstand stood on the wall opposite. It was slightly larger than other servants' rooms, and there was no evidence the housekeeper would be required to share.

"Do you really think we will find keys lost for a hundred years?" Maxim said. "I'm certain they would have searched Waithe Hall from top to bottom."

Examining the washstand, she said, "But we have never searched for them."

"How are we different?"

"Because we are Alexandra and Maxim."

"Yes," he said. "That is a given. I don't believe, however, being us is accounted a prerequisite for investigation by most."

"We are good at discovering things when we are together. We discovered that pirates' treasure."

"Three—*possibly* silver—coins."

"The Roman artefacts."

"An arrowhead. That may have been Pict in origin."

"The fairy mound."

"That was just a slightly raised clod of dirt."

She made a face. "You are no fun, you know this, don't you?"

Smirking, he crossed his arms over his chest. "But you love me anyway."

Ignoring the race of her heart, she sniffed. She measured the washstand with her step and— she frowned. "Do you think the room is too small?

Uncrossing his arms, he glanced at one wall, and then the wall opposite. He took strides across the room, then disappeared into the hall.

He popped back. "It's two strides short."

Excitement began to build inside her. "Which side?"

Looking between the walls, he pointed. "That one."

Wallpaper covered the wall, peeling at the seams to reveal yellowing plaster. Alexandra ran her fingers over it, noting the difference between the paper and the plaster.

Maxim did the same, his brows drawn in concentration. "Here," he said.

The portion he referred to was more discoloured, the wallpaper slightly sunken. He prodded it, moving about in slight increments.

A crack sounded, and then a portion of the

wall shuddered open. They exchanged glances. She had no idea a passageway was hidden in the housekeeper's room, and judging by the surprise on his face, neither had Maxim.

Silently, he lit the lamp and entered. With butterflies jumping in her stomach, Alexandra followed. The passage was cramped, a narrow, dank corridor extending between the walls. Maxim had to stoop, hunching his shoulders as his head almost brushed the ceiling. The wooden plank floor was liberally coated with dust, their footsteps creating a haze that tickled at her nose.

"There's a staircase," he said.

She peered past him. A railing disappeared into the darkness, the stairs appearing rickety and broken in places. "I do not know we should attempt that."

"At least if we die, none shall find our bodies."

She gave him a sour look. "How is that comforting?"

He bussed her temple. "Come, Alexandra. Where's your spirit of adventure?"

"Possibly at the bottom of that staircase, along with my dignity and, apparently, our never-to-be-found bodies." Bumping his hip with hers, she took a breath. "Fine. If we die, I will blame you."

"Fair enough," he said cheerfully.

The staircase groaned under their weight but did not, mercifully, collapse. In a matter of moments they had traversed it, and she could breathe once more.

The passage extended not much further from the staircase, where it just ended. There was no obvious door, no switch, no lever, nothing to suggest an exit.

"Is that it?" Stymied, she turned to Maxim. "Do you think it a dead end?"

"It can't be." He started knocking the wall. "Why even bother with a passage if it just ends?"

"Who knows why your ancestors did anything?"

"True." One knock sounded hollower than the others. Lifting the lamp higher, Maxim rapped it again. "What's this?"

Almost hidden by accumulated years of grime, the wooden panel was smoother, shinier than those surrounding it.

Alexandra ran her thumbnail around the crease. "Ugh, this is disgusting."

"You could have used one of your tools instead of your nail."

"The tools are in the housekeeper's room." The panel flicked open, and she pulled back in surprise.

"Is there a lever?" Maxim asked.

"Not that I can see. Hold the lamp up?"

Light shone into the small hole as he did so. Though she couldn't see the bottom, for some reason she thought it wouldn't be deep— In the darkness, something glinted. Cautiously, she reached a hand inside.

Peering over her shoulder, Maxim asked

conversationally, "Aren't you afraid of things that bite?"

She shot him a dirty look, but he simply smirked in return. Mumbling under her breath of all the ways she could kill him, she reached farther only to have her fingers brush something cool. Metallic. Excitement rioted within her, her heart racing as her breath locked in her chest.

Slowly, she drew her hand out, unable to believe what she held until she saw it with her own eyes. Uncurling her fingers, they bent over her hand.

There nestled in her palm, shining dully in the light, were a set of keys.

Elation filled her. "We found them!"

A frown drew Maxim's brows. "Why would they have been there?"

Turning the keys in her hand, she examined them. "I don't know. Maybe she dropped them."

"In a secret wall panel?"

"I don't know, Maxim. All I know is we found them. We found them!"

Maxim stared at the keys. Frown melting away, a muscle ticked in his jaw. "We did," he said flatly.

"Do you know what this means, Maxim? It means the story is corroborated. The housekeeper probably lost the keys on a journey to her room and didn't notice. All this time, they've been missing, but now they've been found. She might finally be at peace. Isn't that exciting?"

"Yes."

"I shall have to write a paper for submission to the Spiritualist Society. This warrants greater investigation, and I shall have to organise a more in-depth study." She hugged herself, exuberant at the possibilities. "The observers of the phenomena will all need to be interviewed, and of course I shall have to interview Roxwaithe and perhaps Lord Stephen for their observations of activity throughout the year. How is it no one discovered this before us?"

"I do not know. You are ridiculously capable at discovering things."

"What? No."

"You are. It took you, what, a day and a half to determine what the cause of the ghost rumours were?"

"Three. It took three days. And that was training, and a little luck."

"You have discovered a new passageway."

"It was a dead end. Besides, you helped."

"You found me."

Her heart melted. "I did, didn't I?" she said softly.

He smiled, the expression strangely wistful on his strong face.

The keys weighed heavy in her hand. "And you, Maxim, you shall have to be involved. Not only are you a most excellent assistant, but you could provide invaluable insight into both the history and the current investigation. After all, why were the keys there? Did another servant steal them? Was Margaret Howard framed? Was it even Margaret Howard? Maybe it was directed at another person. Goodness, there are so many possibilities."

The smile faded from his features. "When do you plan to leave Waithe Hall?"

"I'm not sure. Maybe tomorrow?" There was so much to do. She needed to write letters, organise transport, have her clothing shipped to Bentley Close.

He nodded sharply. "Tomorrow."

Mind racing, she started back up the stairs. There was so much to do. She was halfway up the stairs before she realised he wasn't with her. Placing her hand on the balustrade, she turned. He still stood before the panel. "Are you coming?"

He glanced up at her, an unreadable expression on his features. "Yes." Demeanour quiet, he started up the stairs.

His gloom cast a pall upon her excitement. "Is aught wrong, Maxim?"

"No. Why would anything be wrong?"

"I do not know. That is why I asked."

"Nothing is wrong, Alexandra. I am happy for you." He gave her a tired smile.

"Oh. Good."

He said nothing as they traversed the passageway, as they left the housekeeper's chamber, as she wrote her notes in the library.

And he said nothing as they climbed into bed, as she kissed him, as he fell asleep by her side.

Chapter Ten

MAXIM STARED OUT THE window. Bright sunshine greeted him, the sky an endless blue, the lawn easing into the dark green glade. Gently sloping hills blocked the horizon and, over those hills, was Bentley Close.

Arms folded, he stared at where Bentley Close would be. It wasn't far, not above a half hour's walk. He remembered making that trek many times, sometimes with Alexandra, sometimes because he wanted to see her. A torrent of memories had returned to him, and Alexandra featured prominently in nearly all of them. Investigating the secret passages of Waithe Hall. Fishing at the lake. Playing cricket on a summer's day. Holed up in the library while it snowed outside. He also remembered their townhouses in London and traversing through the connecting attic to sneak into her bedchamber. He remembered running through Hyde Park, holding her items as they shopped on Oxford Street, sharing an ice in Convent Garden. He remembered *her*.

Restlessness turned him from the window to stalk the room. The pile of books on the table beside his chair beckoned, but he couldn't yet bring himself to focus. His attention was scattered, such he couldn't keep two thoughts in his head, and agitation made it feel he would jump out of skin.

And all because Alexandra sat in her chair, a lock of hair twisted around a finger.

Notebook in lap, she scribbled in it of an occasion, her pencil between her teeth as she thought. She hadn't left, even though she'd found the keys, even though there was no reason for her to stay. They'd woken this morning, broken their fast, and she'd taken residence in the library while he'd hauled the sandbags in the conservatory out into the sun to dry. He'd fully expected her to be gone when he returned, or at least with her bag packed and ready to leave, but she'd still been in the library, in her chair, bent over her notebook.

Picking up one of the books, he flipped it open. The words were jumbled and wrong. Frowning, he tried again. Just when he thought it made sense, he lost it. Frustrated beyond measure, he was tempted to throw the book across the room, but that wouldn't fix the problem. It wouldn't fix *him*.

Alexandra scribbled something in her notebook.

He didn't understand why she was still here. Why wouldn't she just *leave*? This was the worst part, the waiting. He knew she would. He knew she would leave, and she wouldn't come back. He'd never ask her to stay. What was the point? He'd lose her, no matter what he did. Even if he went back to London with her, if he attempted society, she would quickly discover how broken and wrong he was. When his brothers saw him again, they would remember their father's words, and he would see pity in their eyes, in *Alexandra's* eyes, and they would stay with him because it was bad form to abandon a fool, but he would know, he would *know* that was the only reason they stayed, and he would resent them, and they would resent him, and he'd rather she just left *now* and be done with it.

God damn it, why wouldn't she leave? "I won't go to London," he said abruptly.

She blinked. "Very well," she said, and returned to her notes.

She wasn't listening. "I mean it. I have no desire to move amongst society."

A crease forming on her brow, she looked up. "Neither do I."

His chest felt tight. Why was it so tight? "I will tell my brothers, but that is the extent of it. I may even tell them by letter."

"Your brothers will be pleased. However, I would suggest telling them in person." She pursed her lips. "Actually, perhaps send a letter before you appear. I should think it would be less shocking that way."

He stared at her. She didn't *understand.* "But I won't return to London. I will stay here."

"I have already agreed." She looked back at her notebook. "I don't think these notes are detailed enough. Do you think this requires further explanation?" She held out her notebook.

He looked at the notebook, then he looked at her. "I can't read that."

The words were stark between them. Setting his jaw, he dared her to comment.

"Of course you can," she finally said.

"No. The letters will jumble. I cannot read," he said flatly.

"Right." Folding her notebook closed, she rose from her chair and went to the desk.

He followed her, restlessness biting him. "What are you doing?"

"Getting a piece of paper," she said calmly.

God *damn*, he was spoiling for a fight, and she wouldn't oblige. "I can *see* that. Why?"

"I wish to write a letter to our family physician. I am certain he can assist with your affliction."

"I am not ill. I am defective."

She expelled a breath. "Honestly, Maxim, I do not know where you get such notions. You are not defective."

"My father said I was," he forced out.

"I have no doubt your father regretted his words as soon as he said them."

"I cannot be fixed, Alexandra."

She scribbled something on the page before her. "I never said you could be. But if you can't, we can find a way to work with it."

"I cannot, Alexandra. I cannot inflict this on others. My brothers will resent me. *You* will resent me. You will grow to loathe me, and you will abandon me." His throat tightened. "You are not to abandon me."

"I should never abandon you, Maxim," she said distractedly. "I should think the medical colleges in Edinburgh would be the first place to start, don't you? George often reads their journals and he is forever spouting nonsense about this study or that. Perhaps I should write George first. What do you think?" She looked at him expectantly.

He stared at her. She continued to look at him, as if what she had said had not shattered worlds. Had not shattered his world.

He looked at the books. At her pen poised over the paper. At her.

"I love you," he said.

"I know," she said. "But do you think I should write George?"

He stared at her in disbelief. Something inside him cracked and his knees gave out. Collapsing into his chair, he started to laugh.

She was out of her seat in a flash and before him. "Maxim. Are you well?"

Still laughing, he shook his head. A weight inside him had lifted, and everything seemed right for the first time in years. Since the last time he was with her. Only she would try to help him. Only she had the power to make him think she could.

"Maxim?"

Shaking his head again, he wrapped his arms about her waist and buried himself in her.

Her hand feathered over his hair. "Maxim?"

Closing his eyes, he asked, "Do you love me?"

"Of course." Her hand passed over his hair again. "Are you well?"

"Yes, I—" Cursing himself, he shook his head again. "I am an idiot."

She kissed the top of his head. "As long as you can admit it."

God, he could admit it. He could, because she was with him. Because she loved him. Because, he knew, she didn't think him stupid. "How was I without you for so long?"

"Well, you were in America and you couldn't remember anything," she said. "That more than likely had something to do with it."

This woman. All his life, it had been her. "You have to marry me," he said.

"You know, I think I might," she said slowly. She threaded her fingers through his hair. "I have missed you."

"I have missed you." Tugging her down to him, he captured her lips, telling her without words she was all, she was everything, and he was so glad she put up with his nonsense. Another tug and she was in his lap, cradled in his arms as he kissed her and kissed her.

With a sigh, she rested her head on his shoulder, taking his hand in hers. He watched as she played with his hand, measuring their palms, lacing their fingers. "You are not to think yourself stupid, you know. We can work on it. I've seen you with the books. The desire is there. We will conquer this."

He ducked his head. Her hair smelled of lemons and sunshine. How, he had no clue. "I should go to my brothers, shouldn't I?"

"Yes."

His lips twitched. "Not even going to argue, are you?"

"No." She turned to face him more fully. "They are your family. They deserve to know. Besides, everyone needs their family."

"*You* need your family, because your parents are normal and your siblings love you. I'm not sure I need mine."

"Your brothers might surprise you."

"Doubtful." But it didn't mean he shouldn't try. Especially as she was with him.

They were silent a moment. "Will you stand beside me?" he asked.

Their gazes met. She took his hands in hers. And then she smiled. He felt it all the way to the bottom of his soul. "Always."

Epilogue

Northumberland, England, April 1835

THE GARDENS AT WAITHE Hall were in full bloom. Spring had bludgeoned Northumberland, flowers and blossoms rioting aggressively across the dales to bob gently in the warm breeze.

Tossing the cricket ball from hand to hand, Charlotte scowled at her cousin. "Holly, you are not paying attention."

Holly started. "What?" Then, clearly remembering her manners and they would more than likely be forced to be ladies when they grew up, amended, "Pardon?"

Charlotte brandished the ball. "I could have thrown this at your head and you would have been none the wiser until you were laid flat on the ground, unconscious."

"If you had laid me out, unconscious, I would still be none the wiser."

Holding the ball in one hand, Charlotte

crossed her arms and scowled. "That's neither here nor there."

Holly made no reply, instead smirking horribly and generally being wholly disagreeable. She completely ignored the fact she had been disagreeable in turn.

Folding her arms, Charlotte's other cousin rolled her eyes. "Holly never pays attention," Davina announced.

"Oh, you *are* here, Davina? I could have sworn you were a tree. You're certainly rooted to the spot like one," Holly said snidely.

Davina stuck out her tongue.

Their families had gathered at Waithe Hall to celebrate her, Davina and Holly's birthdays. They would turn thirteen within days of each other, and their families always used it as an excuse to spend time at the ancestral seat of the Earl of Roxwaithe, Holly's father and her and Davina's uncle. Their grandparents were in attendance at Bentley Close, along with aunts and uncles and cousins from her mother's side. They made the short walk to Waithe Hall most days, but tomorrow was the birthday party and all would be in attendance, along with the friends she, Davina and Holly had invited.

For now, they were occupying themselves with a rousing game of cricket. They'd found the cricket bat, stumps and ball amongst other playthings in the nursery and so far, Charlotte had smashed the ball for six and come within a hairsbreadth of shattering a window pane. Not to be outdone, Holly had come perilously close to having to fish the ball from the lake when a particularly impressive turn at the crease had seen her pile on three fours and two sixes in an innings. She'd been overenthusiastic on her last whack, the ball careening wildly over silly mid-on toward the water's edge. Luckily, a bunch of reeds had stopped the ball in ankle-deep water and it had been easily retrieved. Davina had elected to field and had spent the game standing in one spot, arms crossed and examining her nails.

Currently, they were happily sledging each other as Charlotte stepped up to the crease opposite Holly to bowl.

"You couldn't hit this ball if you tried," Charlotte called, tossing said ball from one hand to another.

"I will hit the ball and, what's more, I will smash another six," Holly boasted.

Gaze glued to her nails, Davina snorted.

Charlotte smirked. "I should like to see you try."

"I shall try as hard as Aunt Alexandra tried to find the Sewell ghost last night."

Charlotte drew in her breath. Her mother was a noted spiritual hunter and scholar, and no matter what Holly said, her mother was *brilliant*. "You take that back."

Even Davina had glanced up, her eyes wide as she stared at their cousin.

"No," Holly gloated.

Casting about for something equally heinous to say, she grasped something her brother had told her only yesterday. "Your father cried when my father returned," she taunted.

Holly gasped. "He did not," she said indignantly.

"He did. He was so happy Papa was not dead, he wept."

"Now I know you're fibbing. *An earl does not weep*," Holly quoted, no doubt having heard her father say so on numerous occasions.

Stubbornly, Charlotte shook her head. "He did weep. And Uncle Stephen, too."

"Uncle Stephen cries at the drop of a hat," Holly dismissed.

"Don't speak of my father that way," Davina demanded.

Holly shot her an impatient look. "He *does* cry at the drop of a hat."

"There's nothing wrong with that!" Davina glared at her, and Holly's breath exploded in a dismissive puff of air.

"Well, that day he cried because of my father," Charlotte said. Everyone knew the story. Her father had been lost at sea, and everyone had thought him dead. Then, he'd returned to England, her mother had discovered him, told him he was a blockhead for hiding, and they'd all lived happily ever after. Well, apart from the fact where they'd burdened her with both older *and* younger brothers. Honestly, who has *sons*? One brother should have been quite enough, especially as after they'd had that one, they'd had the good sense to have her.

She looked over at her parents. Her mother stood with her father, their hands almost touching. They always stood so close, and they constantly touched one another. Every morning, her father would greet her mother at the breakfast table with a kiss, as if they hadn't just left the same bedchamber. It was romantic, she supposed, and maybe one day she should like a husband with whom she could do the same, but she should never do so in front of their *children*. It really was completely unnecessary.

"Do you think they'll kiss?" Davina said.

Charlotte made a rude noise. "Ugh, probably. They are forever doing that at home, I cannot think why they should not do it elsewhere." She glanced at Holly slyly. "Much like the earl and the countess."

Holly flushed. "Do not speak of my parents in that way."

Davina laughed, and Charlotte grinned as she bowled the cricket ball at Holly.

They were in the midst of a rather invigorating innings of cricket when up the hill trudged her brother. James had found a branch from somewhere and employed it as a walking stick, stabbing it into the ground with every step. He wasn't alone, though, and Charlotte got a strange catch in her chest as Nicholas met her gaze, his smile cheeky as he winked at her. Two years her senior, her brother's best friend had always just *been* there. However, at some point over the summer, she had become intensely...*aware* of him, such she always knew when he had entered a room, and she stammered and acted like a bufflehead when he got near. For some reason, all had changed and now he made her breathless and tingly, and she would really rather it stop but, it seemed, it was only worsening with time. It was deuced annoying.

"You've gone red," Davina remarked.

"What? No, I haven't. *You're* red," she said.

Davina's brows almost shot off her face, and the most horrible smirk lit Holly's features.

Ducking her head, Charlotte ignored them both, ignored James as he approached, and she definitely ignored Nicholas.

"I think you like him," Holly whispered loudly.

"Shush," she hissed. He hadn't heard, had he? Oh goodness, please let it be he hadn't heard. Her mother often said she'd known her father was the one for her, that they'd been friends their entire lives and had not been apart, except for when her father was lost. Her mother had said she'd looked at him upon his return and just *known*.

Charlotte had a horrible feeling she'd experienced the same thing.

"Hello, Charlotte," Nicholas called, and the grin on his face made it so she knew, *she knew*, he had heard.

She swallowed, knowing her cheeks were

flaming red. "Hello, Nicholas."

He stopped before her, a lunatic grin on his face.

"How are you today?" she said politely.

"I am well," he said. "Charlotte?"

"Yes?" She just wanted to sink into the ground. Right now.

"I'm going to marry you one day."

She gaped like a fish. "I...Sorry...What?"

He kissed her cheek. "One day," he said, and she shivered.

And, one day, after she'd made him work for it because she had *some* self-respect, he did.

Acknowledgments

Thank you to my wonderful family and amazing friends who have been so fantastically supportive on this journey. Thank you for taking the magnets when forced upon you, for listening to my moaning, and for letting me vent when I needed it.

Thank you, as always, to my phenomenal critique partner, editor and F4E, A. L. Brady.

Thank you to you, the reader, for embracing Alexandra and Maxim. Look for RESCUING LORD ROXWAITHE, the next in the Lost Lords series, and STEALING LORD STEPHEN, the epic conclusion.

Read the next book in the Lost Lords series

RESCUING LORD ROXWAITHE

The girl he's always loved
Oliver, Earl of Roxwaithe, has always regarded Lady Lydia Torrence as a sibling even as she'd declared one day they would wed. Fourteen years her elder, Oliver was convinced Lydia felt only a crush and when she inevitably declared her love, he had to refuse. After she left for the Continent, he told himself he didn't miss her, that she had always been too young, and if perhaps he'd noticed she had become a woman, that was best left unsaid.

The man she's always adored
Lydia had always known she loved Oliver and he loved her. Furious he would claim she was too young, she determined to take the Continent by storm, to hone her skills and become an expert in flirtation. Upon her return to London, she'd show him she was a fully-grown woman who knew what she wanted—and she wanted him.

Oliver is stubborn in his resolve until a new suitor for Lydia puts Oliver's resolve to the test. Will he discover the girl he's always loved has become the woman he will forever adore?

Read an Excerpt from
RESCUING LORD ROXWAITHE
Lost Lords, Book Two

Chapter One

Roxegate,
London, England,
July, 1819

HE'D READ THE SAME sentence three times.

Pinching the bridge of his nose, Oliver focused on the report before him and ignored the complaints of his stomach. He'd been at his desk since seven o'clock that morning, and he'd only just realised he'd missed lunch. Par for the course, really. His staff knew not to disturb him when the study door was shut and would no doubt deliver a larger dinner to make up for the shortfall, if he remembered to make his way to the dining room. Perhaps he should take a small break and ring for a footman to deliver a sandwich or some such, but from the corner of his eye he saw the towers of reports and papers his secretary had left this morning and discarded it as the wishful thinking it was.

Exhaling, he leant his head on the back of his chair and looked out the window, resolving to ignore his stomach. Outside it was murky and grey, but when was London not murky and grey? The murky afternoon would pass into a murky evening, and then turn to a murky morning. London was nothing if not consistent. The street lamp outside the window would soon be lit, and then carriages against cobblestones would rumble past as society travelled to their amusements for the evening.

He'd remain in his study and work, as he had most evenings for the past year and a half. He couldn't remember the last time he'd attended a gathering of society, apart from the occasional dinner at Torrence House or with Wainwright and his lady. There was too much to do and there was little to tempt him to abandon it.

Without him realising, his gaze had strayed to the chair by the fireplace and the stack of books on the table beside it.

Jerking his gaze back where it belonged, Oliver leant over the report open on his desk. This one was from the steward of Waithe Hall, the usual quarterly report. He could count on one hand the number of times he'd been to Waithe Hall since becoming the earl but he'd not stayed there, instead staying at Bentley Close, the neighbouring estate owned by the Marquis of

Demartine. Waithe Hall held too many ghosts.

Exhaling steadily, he glanced at the report and his gaze snagged on an odd phrase. Frowning, he reread the passage. The villagers of Waithe Village were still reporting strange lights troubling Waithe Hall, and the report claimed wild stories rioted in its wake. The villagers spoke of ghosts and ghouls, with a particular favourite being the old legend of a housekeeper of Waithe Hall roaming in search of her lost keys. He remembered as children, Alexandra and Maxim would search the hall for her keys and—

He drew in his breath. A dull ache pained him at the thought of his lost brother.

Shaking himself, he closed the report. He'd mentioned this phenomenon to Lord Demartine last month, but the earl had dismissed the report as so much talk, citing the Hall's history of ghost stories that always amounted to nothing.

His gaze again strayed to the chair opposite. Jerking it away, he focussed on a report of the Roxwaithe shipping concern. They'd come close to losing another shipment on the passage around South Africa, treacherous waters and pirates doing their utmost to inflict damage. Lord Demartine had been right in his advice, however. The employ of a master navigator and a host of security staff had taken care of both concerns. Lord Demartine often said to make money one had to spend money, and the adage had proved true once more.

Pinching the bridge of his nose again, he

exhaled. At least he had no parliamentary concerns. The summer session had ended the week previous, though he would remain in London through autumn and most of winter. Perhaps in the new year he would visit the Penzance estate. Lord and Lady Demartine were due to tour the Continent, and their offspring would more than likely remove to Bentley Close in the coming months. There would be nothing in London bar work, and he could do that by the sea as well as he could do it in the capital.

The door to his study opened. "I am not ready, Rajitha," he said. "Come back in an hour."

"Roxwaithe?"

His head jerked up.

Instead of his secretary, a woman stood in the doorway. Light from the large windows in the entrance hall outlined her form and cast the rest of her in shadow. For a moment, for half a second, his heart beat faster and an inexplicable joy crashed through him. Then she stepped forward.

She wasn't as tall, and her hair was blonde instead of a reddish kind of gold. Her dress was a sensible shade of cream, and she wore a mint green spencer, the short jacket suggesting she had traversed the street between their houses rather than clamber through their shared attic.

It wasn't disappointment he felt. Of course it wouldn't be her.

Standing, he greeted Lydia's sister. "Lady Alexandra."

"Lord Roxwaithe." At his gesture, Alexandra seated herself in the chair before his. "How are you?"

"I am well." This was odd. He couldn't recall Alexandra had ever entered his study, unlike Lydia, who had burst through the door more times than he could possibly recall. "And you? Your family?"

"I and they are well. My mother asks after you and invites you to dine with us Wednesday next."

"I should be delighted to attend." It was a strange circumstance with Alexandra. He'd know her since her birth but she always brought to mind his brother. As children, she and Maxim had been joined at the hip and no matter the years that had passed since his death, the sight of Alexandra Torrence brought a deluge of memories and with them, a wave of grief. "Will it be family only?"

She nodded. "Though my middle brother is still on tour. George is in Prague. We receive letters from him on occasion, and always filled with the most excruciating details. Apparently, he has discovered a history of grotesquery in an abandoned medical clinic outside Karlin."

Oliver concealed a smile. The Torrences had always had odd interests and George, true to their nature, was obsessed with the medical and sought out grotesqueries across the Continent. "How many clinics is that now?"

"Four." Her lips twisted ruefully. "One

would almost believe my brother to be searching them out rather than educating himself on history and art."

"And your other brothers?"

"They are both well. Preparations for Harry's wedding proceed, and Michael is doing well at Eton."

"I am glad to hear it."

She smiled. The fire crackled, and in the distance, he could hear the movements of his staff as they went about their duties outside the study.

"My sister is also well," Alexandra finally said.

He told himself his interest in Lydia was no different than any other who was acquainted with her. "Is she?"

"Since her return from the Continent, she has cut a broad swathe through the Ton. Papa has had to wade through all the gentlemen wishing to court her."

Dull pain lodged in his chest as he made a noncommittal noise. He was too young for heart problems. Maybe it was because he hadn't eaten.

He knew Lydia had returned. Three months ago. She'd toured Paris, Venice, and Vienna for a year and a half, and he'd braced himself for seeing her for the first time since her eighteenth birthday ball. He'd needn't have bothered as it had been, by anyone's reckoning, anticlimactic. He'd attended a family dinner at Torrence House, and his palms had sweated and his heart had raced, but when she had spied him, her gaze had slid over him with a polite smile as if there were nothing between them. As if she hadn't said she'd loved him. In the months since her return, she'd spoken all of four words to him, and only then after he'd welcomed her home. *Thank you, Lord Roxwaithe.*

"She'll be at the Fanning ball tonight," Alexandra said.

His hands curled into fists. "Along with most of London," he said as indifferently as he could. "Forgive me, Lady Alexandra, but what brings you to Roxegate?"

Sitting back in her chair, she asked, "I cannot visit an old family friend?"

"You have not done so before," he said bluntly. "How can I assist you?"

She bit her lip. "My father told me of a report. From Waithe Hall."

Of course. The Torrences had peculiar interests. Her brother was interested in medical grotesquery, her sister in tying men in knots, and Alexandra Torrence was interested in the occult.

"Father won't expand upon it, but you will, won't you, Roxwaithe?" She looked at him beseechingly.

He didn't know how to respond. At more than one house party, Alexandra searched its rooms and halls for evidence of ghostly visitation. Lord Demartine spoke with pride of the lexicon Alexandra had gathered, and encouraged his eldest daughter in her pursuits. The Torrences were, as previous, uniformly odd.

They were, however, his family. He and Stephen had leaned heavily on the Torrences when Maxim had died, and when he'd become the earl, Lord Demartine's council had steered him from disaster too often to count. It was strange Lord Demartine did not wish to encourage Alexandra in this particular pursuit, but he would not go against the Marquis's wishes. "I am sorry, Lady Alexandra," he said quietly.

"It is only it is such an interesting circumstance, and I have a personal connection to Waithe Hall. I already know all the tales and…."

"Waithe Hall is closed, Alexandra. No doubt it is simply the villagers' imaginations."

"No doubt," she echoed. "You will tell me, though, should there be any more reports?"

"I will discuss them with your father, and relay to him any necessary impact to Bentley Close."

"That's not what I—" She sighed. "Thank you, Roxwaithe." Getting to her feet, she gave him a small smile. "I shall trouble you no further and leave you to your work."

Hastily, he rose. "It was no trouble."

She gave another smile and turned to leave.

Unable to stop himself, he said, "Your family are to the Fanning ball tonight?"

She paused, clearly surprised. He didn't blame her. "Yes. Will we see you there, my lord?"

Of course he wouldn't attend. He never

attended balls anymore. "Yes," he said, surprising even himself.

A frown troubled her brow briefly. "I hope you will seek me out."

Remembering his manners, he said, "And that you shall save me a dance."

"Of course. No need to see me out," she said as he stepped from behind his desk.

He hovered awkwardly. "But—"

"We are practically family."

They were. Lord Demartine was more of a father to him than his ever had been.

"Good day, my lord." Alexandra left, closing the door quietly behind her.

Slowly, he lowered himself into his chair. He never went to balls anymore. Hell, had he even responded to the invitation?

He rang for his secretary and Rajitha was, as always, prompt in his response. "Yes, my lord?"

"Rajitha, did I respond to the Fanning invite?"

It took Rajitha but a moment to respond. "No, my lord."

"In that case, do so now in the affirmative and extend my apologies to Lady Fanning for the lateness of my reply."

"Yes, my lord. Do you require anything further?"

"Not at the moment. Thank you, Rajitha."

The secretary offered a short bow and departed.

Leaning back in his chair, Oliver stared

again out the window. Why he'd agreed to go to the ball baffled him. He'd only been to a handful of gatherings in the last year; he had been busy, and he hadn't wanted to make things awkward for her. For Lydia. After the dinner where she'd ignored him, he'd barely seen her, mostly by design. She clearly had no wish to renew their friendship and he had no desire to force his presence where it wasn't wanted. She'd obviously realised her actions on her eighteenth birthday had been a mistake and if her determined pursuit of other men was any indication, she had realised all she had felt was a crush. Theirs had always been an unusual friendship, and it was always a given she would grow out of it. It was for the best, really. No doubt one day soon he would be holding the invitation to her wedding.

Belatedly, he looked down at his fist. How odd. The paper within it was crushed. Methodically, he smoothed the paper, making it line up with the others on his desk.

The ball tonight could be interesting. Perhaps he should start the search for a bride. Lydia was cutting a swathe through the Ton, perhaps he could do the same. He would be thirty-five on his next birthday and though he had Stephen as his heir, his brother also had yet to marry and set up his nursery.

He stared down at the creased paper. It would be fine to see her tonight. Maybe they would even share a dance and, maybe, they would again be friends. Maybe she would tell him of her adventures, and she would laugh and tease him as she always had, and things would be…normal.

Shaking himself, he turned back to his work. Maybe was a dangerous word. Maybe was hope and desire, and could lead to disappointment as much as anything. He would attend the ball and maybe, if he was lucky, it would be unremarkable.

Chapter Two

FROM THE BALCONY, LYDIA stared into darkness. Behind her, the sounds of the Fanning ball drifted into the night: laughter and music, crystal clinking and conversation. A warm breeze lifted the curls lying against her nape, playing her hair gently against her skin.

Closing her eyes, she allowed London to wash over her. She'd enjoyed her time on the Continent immensely but she'd missed the country of her birth, and now she'd returned she took every opportunity to soak in that which made England. There was nothing quite like the capital on a summer's eve, with the threat of a thunderstorm brewing in the distance and the scent of honeysuckle and lilies carried on the breeze.

"Here you are." Lord Matthew Whitton leaned one shoulder against the door jamb, a rakish smirk on his handsome face.

Placing her elbows against the balustrade, she returned his smile. All evening they'd sent each other glances and it seemed the game they'd played had now come to a head. "Here I am."

"I thought to offer you my arm and a dance, Lady Lydia."

"Did you?" Amusement filled her as he frowned, clearly not expecting such a dismissive response. However, he recovered quickly, his face once more wreathed with a rakish grin.

"I did, but I am much taken with this interaction instead," he said. "There is nothing more beautiful than a lady bathed in moonlight."

"Any lady, sir? One would think a certain specificity in this situation would be warranted."

A frown touched his brow before it smoothed again, his smile seductive. "Of course I am referring to you, Lady Lydia. There is none in London who can rival your beauty."

"Only London? Fie, I did hope for a greater reach."

Again, consternation. Inwardly, she sighed. She found her countrymen had not the skill of the French or the wit of the Viennese.

Eventually, comprehension lit his gaze that she sought to further their game. "I am covered in blushes to have been so gauche as to suggest such, my lady. I have not yet been further than our own fair country, and so did not think to compare beauties in other lands. Forgive me."

"But of course, sir. It is an easy mistake to make."

He grinned broadly. "You are quite jolly, aren't you?"

Disappointment filled her. "Lord Matthew, you do not abandon a flirtation in the middle. When you do make it to Paris and beyond, the ladies will be most disappointed."

"I have other skills."

She watched as he came closer. Raising his hand, he lifted a curl from her nape and twined it around his finger. "Shall I show you?"

"It is of supreme discourtesy to offer such a thing and then not display it."

The corner of his lip lifted. "So shall I?"

Her response was to simply raise a brow.

Slowly, he bent his head and his lips brushed hers, gentle and sweet. What would be his next move? Would he believe, because she'd agreed to a kiss, she'd agree to more? Or was he a sensible boy, and realise a woman agreeing to a kiss meant just that?

It seemed he was a sensible boy. His lips moved against hers, long dark lashes resting against his cheeks. It was so unfair. Why did men always have the beautiful lashes? Her own were stubby things, such she'd taken to darkening them with beeswax and soot as her French lady's maid had shown her in Paris.

With a sigh, Lord Matthew pulled back, his arms still caging her to the balustrade. "That was pleasant," he said softly.

It *was* pleasant. Lord Matthew was a pleasant enough fellow, and he seemed to understand the game with minimal prodding. He was at most two years her elder and the heir to the Earl of Cornell. Her family would be pleased should she announce he courted her. There was absolutely no reason she shouldn't fall in love with him.

The loud clearing of a throat interrupted them. Lord Matthew hastily pushed himself from her, his charming smile fading as he paled. Lydia couldn't fault him his reaction. The Earl of Roxwaithe in a cold temper was a terrifying sight.

Jaw clenched, Oliver stood rigid, blocking the entrance to the house. Dark brows drew further over cold grey eyes, noting Lord Matthew still stood closer to her than was proper, while full lips tightened into a displeased line. Long golden brown hair was clubbed back at his nape, and a close-cropped beard shadowed his strong jaw. An immaculately tailored coat clung to wide shoulders that tapered to narrow hips, and buff-coloured breeches covered powerful thighs. She knew, in the past, he'd spent time at Peterson's Gymnasium because whenever she had mentioned it, his cheeks would ruddy and he'd become bashful, so she'd made sure to mention it often. He was half a foot taller than she, towering over most men, and with his hands behind his back, there was little to distract from the awesome breadth of him.

Heart racing, she wet her lips. Damn him, the sight of him still made her weak.

Coldly, Oliver said, "I was unaware you

knew Lady Lydia, Whitton."

"I, ah—" Throwing her a helpless glance, Lord Matthew edged toward the French doors.

Without removing her gaze from Oliver, Lydia said, "I'll see you back in the ballroom, my lord."

"Yes. Thank you," Lord Matthew bowed and departed in haste. He had to edge around Oliver, who stood his ground and watched him silently, eyes glinting in the low light.

When they were alone, she said, "Good evening, Roxwaithe. Are you enjoying the ball?"

"What were you doing with that boy?" he said without preamble.

She shrugged. "Playing."

His expression became colder. "That is your explanation?"

"I wasn't aware I had anything to explain."

"He does not even stay to protect you or ensure your safety. You chose poorly, Lydia."

She sighed. "It was a dalliance, nothing more."

"Even worse. As your elder—"

She laughed without mirth. "Oh yes, please. Do tell me as my elder what I should do."

"As your elder," he continued, as if she hadn't spoken at all. "It behoves me to warn you against playing fast and loose with your reputation."

"It is mine to do with as I please, and no concern of yours."

"Whatever occurred on the Continent, it is

different in London."

"You have no notion of what occurred on the Continent."

His jaw worked. "I see," he said stiffly.

"I'm not sure you do," she retorted. Let him think the worst of her. Let. Him.

Glancing beyond her, he seemingly collected himself. "Regardless of what occurred, you are in London, amongst society. What was permissible in Paris is not here."

"Why are you saying such things to me, as if I do not know the rules? I know them as well as you."

His lips twisted. "Yes. You know them so well you allow a boy to maul you in full view of the ballroom."

"He wasn't mauling me."

"From where I stood, he was certainly mauling you."

"How, pray, was he mauling me? He had both hands on the balustrade." Damnation, but he had no right to interfere. None.

"He was caging you."

"He was not," she retorted.

"I thought he was attacking you!"

"Well, he wasn't!"

The words hung in the night air. Chest heaving, he stared at her, his grey eyes tumultuous. Her chest hurt. How was it they were yelling at each other? Where had it gone so wrong?

Oh, she remembered. When he had rejected

her.

"I apologise," he said.

She turned her face away, willing the tears that burned her eyes to do the same. "Is that all you have to say?"

The gentle breeze picked again at the hair on her nape. In the distance, people laughed and music played.

"I apologise profusely," he finally said.

Bitterness twisted her lips. "Thank you for your condescension, Roxwaithe. I appreciate it greatly."

He frowned. "You're calling me Roxwaithe."

"It is your name. What else should you be called?"

Glancing away, he shrugged.

No. No, he could not do this to her. She would not feel guilty. She wouldn't. "Roxwaithe," she stressed. "Is there aught else you wish to chide me on? My gown, perhaps? The length of my bodice? Perhaps my hair is incorrectly arranged."

His expression hardened. "No. Simply the company you keep."

"Ah, something that has absolutely nothing to do with you. Well done."

He opened his mouth as if he would retort then pressed his lips together. Bowing sharply, he turned on his heel and, before she could say another word, left the balcony.

Crossing her arms, she stared after him. She

wanted to storm after him, grab him and *demand* he pay her attention, but such action had never done her much good, had it? He'd decided to ignore her, and heaven forbid anyone try to change Oliver Farlisle's mind once he'd decided something. It was just like when she'd come back from the Continent. He'd avoided her until he'd been forced to greet her, and then it had been with such an air of disinterest, it had been all she could do to scrounge disinterest in return.

Digging her fingers into her biceps, she forced herself to remain where she was. She'd been so certain they were meant for each other, and the night of her eighteenth birthday had seemed the perfect occasion to show him she was ready. She'd kissed him and, inexperienced though she had been, she'd felt him respond. But then he'd pushed her from him, and the horrified look on his face had almost destroyed her.

When her father had discovered them and sent her to her mother as if she were a child, she'd been so ashamed she'd simply done as he'd commanded. Her mother had been surprised to see her, but when her father had also appeared and, after a few moments of furious whispering, promptly decamped, her mother had turned to her with a wry comprehension.

"So, your father interrupted something," her mother had said.

Pressing her lips together, Lydia hadn't responded.

"Lydia?" her mother had prompted.

Digging her fingers into her biceps, she'd stared at the floor.

Her mother had sighed. "Lydia, were you kissing Lord Roxwaithe?"

Still she hadn't answered.

"Did you kiss him or did he kiss you?"

"What does that matter?" she'd burst out.

"It matters." Her mother had waited.

"I kissed him," she'd finally admitted.

Her mother had sighed again. "I thought so." Her mother had come closer to sit beside her, taking her hand. "Lydia, you cannot force someone to feel as you do."

"I am not forcing him to feel anything. He loves me."

"As a sister—"

"No. He loves me."

Her mother had shaken her head. "Even if he does, he's not ready and you cannot force him."

"*Why* isn't he ready?" she'd asked plaintively. "He's had *years*."

"We do not all wake up at the same time, my love." Her mother had smoothed a curl behind Lydia's ear. "You are yet young, Lydia, and you've seen little of the world. You may have chosen him, but perhaps you should make sure he *is* your choice."

"What do you mean?"

"We have not been to Paris for an age. I will take you. We will shop for your wardrobe and we will attend Parisian society. Perhaps someone will catch your eye."

"No one will catch my eye," she'd said stubbornly.

"Perhaps not, but would you not rather know for sure?"

Exhaling, Lydia rested her forehead on her arms folded on the balustrade. The next day, she'd gone to his study. It had taken every scrap of courage she'd possessed, but she'd resolved to act as if nothing had happened. She could wait. She'd been patient for eighteen years, she could wait a few months more until he came to realise she was a woman grown. However, his study had been locked. She'd stood there dumbly and she'd tried the handle again and it still wouldn't turn. In a daze, she'd returned home. Four days later, she'd been on a ship bound for Paris.

Lydia had done her best to allow someone to catch her eye. She'd been merry and she'd flirted, she'd kissed others and managed to garner a marriage proposal or three. She'd thrown herself into gaiety, pretending she was carefree and her heart had not been claimed before she'd even known what it meant.

Cursing under her breath, she tried to recapture the calm the night afforded her. Damn him. Damn him for destroying her peace. Why could she not rid herself of this? Everyone claimed it was a silly crush. Everyone said she would forget him, that she would fall in love a dozen times before settling on a man to wed. Her friends fell in love with alarming frequency, and each ball offered a new suitor. Why was it she couldn't do the same?

But then...no one else had ever caught her eye.

Using the heels of her hands, she wiped her eyes and, pinching her cheeks, she forced a smile as she left the balcony.

The ball still whirled, even more people adding to its crush. She pushed through the crowd, smiling and laughing and greeting those she knew.

"There you are!" In a cloud of frills and perfume, Lady Violet Crafers appeared at her side. "Lord Seebohm has been asking after you, and Mr Harris was determined to claim his dance."

"I apologise I was not present." She'd missed Violet while she was away. Violet could, and had, filled reams of paper with every *on dit* she came across, but it wasn't the same as watching her friend wildly gesticulate as she reported the latest gossip.

Violet's smile turned sly. "I saw Lord Matthew Whitton follow you."

"Did you?" she said diffidently, knowing it would drive her friend wild.

Violet whacked her with her fan. "Do not give me that. He followed you. What happened?"

Lydia smiled mysteriously.

Violet whacked her with her fan again, her dark curls bobbing. "I knew it! You are a wicked bad woman, Lydia."

"Perhaps, but I am also a woman who knows how Lord Matthew kisses," she said archly.

Violet sucked in her breath. "And?" she asked breathlessly.

"I shouldn't repeat the experience." She deliberately didn't think of the events that followed.

Violet's face fell. "That is disappointing. I always thought he would be good at it."

Lydia shrugged.

"Oh well." Violet smiled sunnily. "Shall we see what refreshments are yet available?"

As they walked from the ballroom and to the refreshment room, Violet chatted steadily, reporting every piece of gossip she'd heard over the last few days. Lydia listened, glad of the distraction. She would not let Oliver ruin her evening. She was here to have fun and by god, fun she would have.

Violet slowed as they approached the refreshments. "Oh," she said in consternation.

"What is it?" Lydia followed her line of sight. Standing at the refreshments, sipping from a crystal glass, stood Seraphina Waller-Mitchell. "Oh."

Violet's lips turned down. "I do not wish to deal with her this evening."

No one in their right mind wished to deal with Seraphina Waller-Mitchell. Seraphina looked down her nose at everyone, whether they were princess or scullery maid or any permutation in between. They were all plebeians to her, and unworthy of her time.

She had, however, decided Lydia was worth her time. At some stage, Lydia had incurred her wrath and she had dedicated herself to singling Lydia out at every occasion. Lydia had no idea why. Seraphina was six years her elder and thus Lydia should have been beneath her notice, yet Seraphina had gone out of her way to make comment on her choice of gown, how she styled her hair, her dancing companion, the way she held her head. Seraphina had an opinion on it all, and all of it snide.

Tonight, Seraphina stood with a punch glass in her hand, her chin arrogantly high as she surveyed the room. Her henchwomen, Maria Spencer and Elizabeth Harcourt, flanked her, the three of them ready to attack whoever was foolish enough to stray near them.

Lydia squared her shoulders. "Come," she said to Violet.

Violet wet her lips. "Do we have to?"

"Do not worry. I will protect you."

A little green, Violet followed as Lydia strode for the refreshment table.

Seraphina Waller-Mitchell smiled at them. "Lady Lydia. Lady Violet. *Such* a delight to see you. And in such...gowns."

How Seraphina Waller-Mitchell turned a smile into an insult was truly a work of art. "And you, Lady Seraphina." Lydia forced herself to say no more, instead picking up a plate and helping herself to a sandwich triangle.

Seraphina watched her with interest while Maria Spencer and Elizabeth Harcourt glared, obviously waiting for Seraphina's direction.

Lydia ignored them, piling sandwich after sandwich onto her plate. She refused to be intimidated, she absolutely refused. The back of her neck prickled, and she ignored the coldness slithering down her spine.

"How are Lord Henry's wedding preparations proceeding?" Seraphina asked suddenly.

"Well," she replied cautiously.

"I am so pleased to hear that."

She wasn't going to ask. This was how Seraphina drew you in. She made a statement and then—

Seraphina smiled thinly. "I knew there was nothing to the rumours."

Don't ask, don't ask, don't—

"What rumours?" Violet asked, and immediately looked to be castigating herself for responding.

"You've not heard the rumours?" Seraphina asked, her tone arch. Maria Spencer exchanged a knowing look with Elizabeth Harcourt, who simply smirked.

Lydia grit her teeth. This was what Seraphina did, she reminded herself. She cast doubt with baseless rumour.

Seraphina's expression brimmed with false sympathy. "I am certain there is nothing in them, absolutely certain."

"There is nothing wrong with Harry and Tessa," Violet burst out.

Silently, Lydia regarded Seraphina.

The other woman met her gaze, the corners of her lips lifting slightly. "No. Of course not. Nothing at all."

Maria and Elizabeth watched breathlessly while Lydia held Seraphina's gaze, refusing to yield to the woman.

"I'll bid you good evening, Lady Seraphina. I do hope you enjoy the ball," Lydia finally said, as calmly as she could manage.

"I shall, Lady Lydia. You may rely upon it." Seraphina said with a smile that would slice one so precisely, one wouldn't realise one bled until five paces away.

Taking Violet's elbow, Lydia led them away. Her skin thrummed, and she wanted quite illogically to smash something.

"Oh, I wish I could just slap that smirk off her face," Violet seethed.

"I know, but we can't. She's horrible, Violet. Don't think on her any longer."

"It's a lie, you know."

"I know."

"Whatever she's heard, it's a lie."

"Most likely she's fishing, or attempting to stir contrary where there is none. I shouldn't think on it, Violet."

"No."

But they both knew they would. "In any

event," Lydia said, "Harry would tell us if there was a worry."

Violet gave her a look. "Lydia," she said. "Harry is a man."

"True," she conceded. "Tessa would tell us. Rumours are not facts, Violet. We should not treat them as if they were."

Violet exhaled. "She just makes me so mad."

She rubbed her friend's arm comfortingly. "Let us enjoy the rest of the ball. We shan't let her taint our evening."

"Agreed." Violet determinedly popped a sandwich in her mouth.

"Who shall we allow to dance with us, do you think?"

A reluctant smile tilted her friend's lips. "Only the most handsome and the most intelligent."

"Both? That will narrow the field considerably." Lydia's gaze wandered over the throng. Oliver was not among them. Most likely he was in the card room with his friend Wainwright. It was how he usually spent his time at a ball and—

She closed her eyes, annoyed at herself. Taking a breath, she forced a smile and, with Violet at her side, she entered the fray.

TEACH ME

by Cassandra Dean

Ever curious, Elizabeth, Viscountess Rocksley, has turned her curiosity to erotic pleasure. Three years a widow, she boldly employs the madam of a brothel for guidance but never had she expected her education to be conducted by a coldly handsome peer of the realm.

To the Earl of Malvern, the erotic tutelage of a skittish widow is little more than sport, however the woman he teaches is far from the mouse he expects. With her sly humor and insistent joy, Elizabeth obliterates all his expectations and he, unwillingly fascinated, can't prevent his fall.

Each more intrigued than they are willing to admit, Elizabeth and Malvern embark upon a tutelage that will challenge them, change them, come to mean everything to them...until a heartbreaking betrayal threatens to tear them apart forever.

SILK & SCANDAL
THE SILK SERIES, BOOK 1

by Cassandra Dean

Eight years ago...
Thomas Cartwright and Lady Nicola Fitzgibbons were friends. Over the wall separating their homes, Thomas and Nicola talked of all things – his studies to become a barrister, her frustrations with a lady's limitations.

All things end.
When her diplomat father gains a post in Hong Kong, Nicola must follow. Bored and alone, she falls into scandal. Mired in his studies of the law and aware of the need for circumspection, Thomas feels forced to sever their ties.

But now Lady Nicola is back…and she won't let him ignore her.

ROUGH DIAMOND
THE DIAMOND SERIES, BOOK 1

by Cassandra Dean

Owner of the Diamond Saloon and Theater, Alice Reynolds is astounded when a fancy Englishman offers to buy her saloon. She won't be selling her saloon to anyone, let alone a man with a pretty, empty-headed grin…but then, she reckons that grin just might be a lie, and a man of intelligence and cunning resides beneath.

Rupert Llewellyn has another purpose for offering to buy the pretty widow's saloon- -the coal buried deep in land she owns. However, he never banked on her knowing eyes making him weak at the knees, or how his deception would burn upon his soul.

Each determined to outwit the other, they tantalize and tease until passion explodes. But can their desire bridge the lies told and trust broken?

About Cassandra Dean

Cassandra Dean is an award-winning author of historical and fantasy romance. She grew up daydreaming, inventing fantastical worlds and marvelous adventures. Once she learned to read (First phrase – To the Beach. True story), she was never without a book, reading of other people's fantastical worlds and marvelous adventures.

Cassandra is proud to call South Australia her home, where she regularly cheers on her AFL football team and creates her next tale.

Connect with Cassandra

cassandradean.com

facebook.com/AuthorCassandraDean

twitter.com/authorCassDean

instagram.com/authorcassdean

bookbub.com/authors/cassandra-dean

To learn about exclusive content, upcoming
releases and giveaways,
join Cassandra's mailing list:

cassandradean.com/extras/subscribe

Made in the USA
Columbia, SC
21 September 2021